"Running away ~~again~~
did s~~~~**

Matt's ~~~~
gaze, an~~~~ ~~~~ ~~~~ but
on her g~~~~

"Just wha~~, ~~ whom, am I supposed to
be running from?"

"Me," he declared evenly, when a few
painfully slow seconds had passed.
"You'd have been wiser to have
stayed in Auckland and faced the
inevitable."

"By inevitable, I suppose you mean
your wearing down my resistance
sufficiently so that you can bed me,"
she accused scathingly. "You'll never
win, Matt. Accept me as the one that
got away."

"My dear Karen," he drawled silkily,
"you're like a little wild kitten, all
claws and bristling soft fur. You hiss at
every hand—regardless."

As his eyes held hers, unwavering in
their scrutiny, Karen knew the battle
was on.

HELEN BIANCHIN

edge of spring

Harlequin Books

TORONTO • LONDON • LOS ANGELES • AMSTERDAM
SYDNEY • HAMBURG • PARIS • STOCKHOLM • ATHENS • TOKYO

Harlequin Presents edition published March 1981
ISBN 0-373-10415-4

Original hardcover edition published in 1979
by Mills & Boon Limited

CHAPTER ONE

'WHAT have you been doing with yourself, darling?'

Karen caught the inquisitive sparkle in her mother's eyes, and endeavoured not to smile. 'Oh, this and that,' she answered lightly. 'I take it you had a smooth drive down from Whangarei? What time did you leave?'

Grace Ingalls took an appreciative sip of tea from the cup she was holding, then gave an expressive sigh. 'I meant to get away soon after breakfast, but Emily rang, and then I couldn't find Simone.' She grimaced ruefully across the table at Karen. 'Honestly, I'm sure that cat knows when I'm preparing to leave her for more than a day's outing. It took me more than an hour to find her—on top of the garage roof, if you please—and then she refused to come down, despite any enticement I offered. In the end, I had to enlist Mr Jenkins' help, and you know how he talks—it was all of thirty minutes before he took his ladder and left. And as if that wasn't enough, the wretched animal miaowed pitifully all the way to the boarding kennels, which had the effect of making me feel I was deserting her for life, instead of a day and a half!'

'Oh, Mother!' Karen burst out laughing, and her vivid blue eyes lit with genuine amusement as she envisaged Grace's Siamese pet effecting feline histrionics. 'Simone has had you wound around her paw from the moment you first brought her home.'

'Well, she's marvellous company,' Grace defended. 'There are times when she's almost human.' She picked up the teapot to refill her cup, added milk and sugar to her satisfaction, then she glanced up to regard Karen with thoughtful contemplation. 'Your letters of late have been newsy oracles, mentioning everything except your social life. I find it difficult to believe you haven't dated anyone at all.'

Karen wrinkled her nose expressively, and offered an unabashed grin. 'Believe, Mother. As strange as it may seem, I actually enjoy staying home, and besides, you know my views on leaving Lisa in the care of a baby-sitter unless it's really necessary.'

'That's all very well, darling, but you must try to go out sometimes,' Grace protested. 'Heavens, you're only twenty-five. One bad experience doesn't necessarily mean you should suffer for the rest of your life.'

' "Once bitten, twice shy", remember?' she couldn't resist taunting, and saw the fleeting frown that appeared as Grace conceded cautiously——

'Yes. But a woman needs a man, like a——'

'Flower needs rain?' Karen completed cynically. 'If that's true, then why haven't *you* remarried?' The instant the words were spoken she felt an immediate sense of remorse. 'I'm sorry, that was uncalled for,' she apologised quietly.

'Your father and I shared a relationship which I doubt could be equalled with another man,' Grace revealed simply. 'Love can be like that. Brad——'

'Doesn't exist any more,' Karen intervened firmly. 'He belongs in the past—a part of my life that I strive very hard to forget.'

Grace began tentatively—'This new job of yours. I don't suppose there's anyone——'

'No,' she denied tolerantly. 'The manager is very much married, the accountant a confirmed bachelor well into his forties, and the clerical staff are all women. The factory workers use a side entrance into the building and have their own canteen—apart from the supervisor and a foreman or two, I haven't met any of them.' A mischievous imp rose to the fore, causing her to offer wickedly, 'Of course, I have yet to meet the head man of Consolidated Electronics—the Director himself. He's been in Europe for the past three months, and is due back next week. However, his office suite is upstairs, so my chances of coming face-to-face with him are extremely rare—especially as I work there only part-time.' She didn't add that one of the foremen had persistently angled for a date, offering no fewer than a dozen invitations, and his presence in the office on some pretext or other had become something of a regular occurrence during the six weeks she'd been with the firm. However, Mike Evans didn't fool her at all. His so-called charm could be summed up adequately in three words—invite, inveigle, into-bed.

'I'd like to see you——' Grace hesitated fractionally, and Karen finished wryly——

'Marry again. Sorry, Mother, but I don't aim to take the plunge. Once was enough.' Oh, if only the telephone would ring, or Lisa——

The melodic chimes of the doorbell sounded—almost in answer to her silent prayer. Saved by the bell, she mocked hollowly.

'Barbara—how nice!' she exclaimed with genuine pleasure as soon as she opened the front door. 'Come in.'

'I haven't called at an inconvenient moment?' the tiny elfin-faced brunette queried anxiously, sweeping a hand to indicate Grace's Mini parked beside the garage. 'I see you have visitors.'

Karen explained with a smile, 'Mother is down for

the weekend. She's taking Lisa back to Whangarei for the school holidays.'

The other girl's face lightened with comprehension. 'Of course, you're working now, aren't you? I won't stay long,' she murmured apologetically as she followed Karen down the hall. 'I came to ask a favour, actually.'

'You'd like me to babysit Tania?' Karen anticipated as they reached the dining-room. 'Mother, I'd like you to meet a friend of mine,' she smiled. 'Barbara Cuthbert—Grace Ingalls. Barbara and I first met over a year ago when our daughters were attending the same kindergarten.'

Barbara murmured a greeting, then smiled at Karen. 'I already have a sitter arranged for Tania. It's Bruce—he was due back this morning, but I've had a telephone call to say he's been delayed and won't now arrive until tomorrow. The problem is that we were supposed to go to a party tonight. Bruce insists I should still attend, but I'm not keen to go alone. I've already telephoned the hostess and explained, and she suggested I might like to bring a girl friend along in Bruce's place. I thought of you,' she ended simply, her expression faintly pleading.

'Of course Karen will go,' Grace intervened quickly before her daughter had a chance to so much as open her mouth.

'Mother—no!' Karen found herself protesting. Besides, she added silently, I don't want to go—not to a party. Participating in sophisticated small-talk with a number of people she'd never met didn't thrill her at all—nor did she relish fending off unwanted advances from members of the opposite sex.

'Nonsense, darling,' Grace refuted sunnily. 'It will

be an excellent opportunity for you to meet people. After all, why not take advantage of me in a baby-sitting capacity while I'm here?'

Oh lord, Karen groaned. What else could she do but give in gracefully? Her usual stock-in-phrase refusal on the grounds of being unable to get a sitter for Lisa couldn't be proffered as an excuse. Barbara was unlikely to stay late, so it would only be for a few hours. 'All right, I'll come,' she agreed. 'What time do you want to leave?'

'About nine,' Barbara conveyed with relief. 'There's nothing worse than being one of the first to arrive at a party. Thanks, Karen—you're an angel.'

That's debatable, Karen decided, considering her feelings at that precise moment. Grace was a darling, and a peer among mothers—if only she could be persuaded not to intervene, for over the past five years she had developed a penchant for matchmaking that had proved embarrassing at times.

'Shall we take my car?' she suggested. 'You didn't mention where the party is being held, but I don't mind driving—however distant it might be.' Besides, it was easier to effect a brush-off if after refusing the offer of a lift home she could add that she had her own means of transport.

'Epsom,' Barbara informed her. 'I'll expect you just before nine. Now, if you'll excuse me, I'll get away. I have things to do to my hair, nails—the usual feminine things,' she explained laughingly.

'Darling, let's go through your wardrobe,' Grace suggested the instant Karen returned from seeing Barbara out, and Karen raised her eyes heavenward in mute appeal.

From now until the minute she left, she'd be subjected to subtly-voiced criticisms and suggestions with regard to her clothes, hairstyle, and make-up.

It took an hour to arrive at the choice of a dress in jersey-silk that blended pastel tonings of pink, lilac and blue, and shortly after seven o'clock Karen showered and slipped into fresh underwear before beginning to apply make-up with care.

Her vivid blue eyes were highlighted with eyeshadow and the skilful application of mascara, and she used a blusher below her cheekbones to give her pale complexion an illusion of colour. Her lips she lightly touched with pink, then added gloss.

Taking the dress from its hanger, she stepped into it and fastened the zipper, then she turned and critically surveyed her reflection. Barbara hadn't divulged whether or not it was a formal or informal affair, but the full-skirted dress was suitable for either occasion.

It turned out to be a prestigious event, with the accent being on carefully-contrived informality. After two hours of smiling pleasantly, Karen began to feel as if she was taking part in a stage play, for none of it seemed quite real.

She glanced idly round the crowded room and attempted to display some interest in the mingling guests spilling out from the large downstairs entertainment room through open glass doors into an adjoining courtyard. Snatches of amused laughter drifted above the steady buzz of conversation, and her attention wandered towards a delicate tracery of ascending cigarette smoke spiralling beneath one of the dimmed lanterns.

All at once a sudden prickle of awareness slithered down her spine, and curious to discover the cause, she turned slightly to encounter a pair of tawny-gold eyes levelled in her direction.

The man was tall, his broad frame expensively sheathed in an impeccably-tailored beige suit, and he emanated virile masculinity from every nerve and fibre. Features were strongly etched in a face too rough-hewn to be termed handsome, and there was an air of decisiveness about him that bordered almost on arrogance.

Disconcertingly frank, his eyes held calculated interest tinged with amusement, and Karen felt herself grow faintly pink beneath their gaze as she watched him cover the short distance between them with a movement that was lithe and deliberately indolent.

'Would you care for a cigarette?' The deep gravelly-drawl held a hint of mockery, and she gave a negative shake of her head.

'I don't smoke, thank you,' she declined politely.

An eyebrow lifted quizzically as he indicated her empty glass. 'Another drink, perhaps?'

He was very sure of himself, she decided wryly. 'I think I've had enough,' she voiced with a slight smile, hoping that he would now drift away.

His eyes roved slowly over her features with dismaying thoroughness before coming to rest on her mouth. 'We haven't been introduced,' he observed musingly. 'I would have remembered.'

'Karen Ingalls,' she murmured, meeting that dark probing gaze squarely. Without conscious thought her eyes slid down to his mouth, and a tiny shiver shook her equilibrium as she imagined the way those sensuously-moulded lips would feel caressing her skin. Dear God, she must be going mad to even contemplate such a thought! Deliberately she forced a smile, acting out a part in this crazy charade.

'You're not playing fair,' she declared with mock

severity. 'Or perhaps you don't possess a name?'

His eyes gleamed with hidden laughter. 'Lucas—Matt Lucas.' Reaching out a negligent hand, he caught hold of her wrist and gently drew her towards him. 'Dance with me, Karen.'

Her mouth pouted captivatingly. 'It's usual to ask, not command.'

White teeth flashed as his lips parted in a sardonic smile. 'Would it help if I say "please"?'

'What a shame I'm immune to your charm, Mr Lucas,' she said sweetly, and felt unusually nettled when he laughed.

'Shall we dance, and aim for an amicable silence?'

It was easier to capitulate than argue, although she wasn't prepared for the strange curling sensation that began in the pit of her stomach when he drew her into his arms, and it slowly spread until her whole body felt tinglingly alive. There was a pull of the senses, a sheer physical magnetism she had thought herself incapable of ever experiencing again, and a shiver of apprehension slid down her spine as she endeavoured to move away from him.

'Cold?'

For some reason her voice seemed to be suffering from a form of temporary paralysis, for the single negative denial had to be forced from her throat. 'No.'

'Afraid?'

Her head jerked back, her body becoming rigid as she strained away from him. 'You flatter yourself!' she vented indignantly, her eyes glittering with anger as she struggled to escape his grasp.

Dark tawny eyes regarded her thoughtfully. 'Why so defensive, Karen?'

'I'm not,' she retorted swiftly. Forcing a brilliant

smile to her lips, she suggested sweetly, 'Why don't you go and enthrall some other female with your—er—charm? I'm sure you'll find someone else more—receptive.'

He allowed her to step back a pace without relinquishing his hold, and his teeth gleamed white as his lips parted in a slow wide smile. Idly he let his hand slip down to her wrist and uncurled her clenched fingers to examine the single gold band with interest. 'Does this bear any significance?'

Unable to believe her ears, Karen gave a startled gasp and snatched her hand away. 'You have no right to—to interrogate me, Mr Lucas!'

'Matt,' he insisted deliberately. 'And you haven't answered my question.'

Her eyes sparked with hidden anger. 'I don't consider I have to!' she flung with asperity. His apparent imperturbability was utterly infuriating.

'Tomorrow evening—will you have dinner with me?'

Oh, the conceit of the man! 'Am I supposed to feel flattered?' she queried icily, meeting his faintly sardonic gaze with disdain. 'Thank you—but no.'

His lips twitched with barely concealed amusement. 'Monday?'

'*No,*' she refused emphatically, and could have hit him when he pursued with quizzical cynicism:

'Tuesday?'

'No—and that applies to all the remaining days in the week!'

After a seemingly interminable silence he chided softly, 'Would having dinner with me constitute such a threat?'

She looked up at him coolly—which was difficult,

when she was boiling inside with angry indignation. 'I don't indulge in sophisticated games, Mr Lucas, and I happen to dislike predatory males.'

'So much hostility, when I haven't so much as put a hand out of place,' he mocked quietly.

'Haven't you anything more amusing to do?' she queried with intended sarcasm.

'Is that what you think I'm doing—amusing myself?'

'Aren't you?' She drew a shaky breath and made an attempt at politeness. 'If you'll excuse me, it's quite late ...' she let her voice trail off deliberately.

'Like Cinderella, at the witching hour of midnight,' he drawled cynically, and she gave a brittle laugh.

'There's little chance my car will turn into a pumpkin. Believe it or not, I'm tired. I'm usually in bed at this hour.'

His eyes crinkled with laughter. 'Karen,' he drawled with intended provocation. 'The image of you in bed is infinitely—disturbing.'

Unbidden, a swift flood of colour tinged her cheeks, lending a rosy hue that was mortifying, and she was unable to prevent the slight trembling of her lips. 'Goodnight, Mr Lucas,' she managed evenly, turning away with the intention of putting as much space between them as quickly as possible, but his hand on her arm prevented her escape.

'Why so formal?'

Karen glared at him with open dislike. 'As we're unlikely to meet again, I hardly think it matters how I address you.' In a minute she'd scream! 'Please let me go.'

'When you've agreed to have dinner with me.'

'Oh!' she uttered wrathfully. 'You would have to be the most egotistical——' She paused in angry indignation, temporarily lost for words. 'You defy description!'

His lips twitched with barely-suppressed humour. 'So I've been told,' he allowed lazily. 'But not in quite the same context to which you allude.'

Karen looked up at him, meeting his gaze steadily. 'I'm sorry, but you're wasting your time.'

'You're not sorry at all, Karen, and,' paused fractionally, 'nothing I do is a waste of time.'

'Then I can only say you're remarkably lacking in perception.'

'Do you think so?'

'Goodnight, Mr Lucas,' she bade coolly. 'I can't say meeting you has been a pleasure.' Without a backward glance she turned and began moving across the room, her eyes circling the guests as she searched for Barbara.

In a matter of seconds she located her, and together they made the necessary farewells to their hostess.

In the car Karen gave a silent sigh of relief. Homeward bound at last.

'Did you enjoy yourself?'

She turned to her companion with a slight smile, assembling a tactful reply as she sent the small Datsun saloon heading towards the main thoroughfare. 'Thank you, Barbara—yes.'

'I saw you succeeded in catching Matt Lucas' eye,' the other girl voiced lightly.

'I wasn't trying to succeed,' Karen declared with droll cynicism, and Barabara shot her a wicked grin.

'Perhaps that's why. He usually has to fight his way free of idolising females. Your coolness would be— intriguing. What did you think of him?'

'What was apparently obvious,' she responded with

a wry grimace, her expressive features wrinkling with
distaste. 'He's a rake—and enjoys the compensations of
being one.' She brought the car to a halt at a set of
traffic lights. 'Thank heavens I won't see him again.'

'I'm afraid you will,' Barbara voiced carefully. 'He
happens to be Matthew J. Lucas, the Director of the
firm you work for—Consolidated Electronics.'

Karen's stomach performed a series of somersaults—
at least it felt like that! It seemed a long time before
she found her voice. 'You're joking—I hope.'

'He flew in yesterday from London.'

Karen closed her eyes momentarily. It didn't seem
fair.

'The lights have changed,' Barbara pointed out, and
with startled realisation Karen engaged the gears.

'Did he ask you out?' Barbara pursued.

'Yes. I refused.'

'That would have whetted his interest,' the other
girl remarked with a slight laugh. 'Wait until he dis-
covers you work for him.'

'He could be Prince Charming and a veritable
Croesus, and I'd still refuse,' Karen declared ruefully.
'And I don't work for him—at least, not personally.
I'm employed as a typist, and part-time at that. His
office is upstairs, complete with a private secretary.
With luck, he won't even notice me.'

'My dear girl, don't you ever look in a mirror?'

The other girl's scandalous tones brought a grimace
to Karen's lips. Of Scandinavian descent, she possessed naturally blonde hair, vivid blue eyes, and a
creamy skin. Six inches above five feet, she was slim
with curves in all the right places. There was a time
when a vivacious personality lent her attractive features a special glow, an inner sparkle that set her apart

from most. But that had been before her marriage to Brad Ellman. Now she preferred a quieter, more serious image.

'Wouldn't you like to remarry, Karen? Surely you can't want to spend the rest of your life alone?'

'I have Lisa,' she said quietly, thankful that they had almost reached the street where Barbara lived. It was only a brief few minutes' drive from there to her own home. 'You'll have to give up on me, Barbara,' she offered lightly as she brought the car to a halt in the illuminated driveway. 'I'm a confirmed cynic where the subject of marriage is concerned.'

'Thanks for collecting me,' Barbara murmured as she slid out from the passenger seat. 'We could just as easily have gone in my car.'

Karen gave a negligible shrug. 'It was easier to use mine, otherwise you would have had to double back more than a mile.'

'Thanks, Karen. We must meet for lunch. One day next week? I'll give you a ring,' Barbara stepped back and gave a friendly wave as Karen reversed the car.

The porch light shone brightly over the front door as she swung the Datsun down towards the garage, and a few minutes later she quietly fitted her key into the lock and closed the door behind her.

'You're back early.'

Karen swung round with a gasp of surprise. 'Mother! Waiting up for me? I don't believe it.'

Grace Ingalls made a slight moue. 'Not exactly, darling, but I couldn't sleep without first hearing how you'd got on. Did you enjoy yourself?'

Oh heavens, it was to be question time with a vengeance! 'Shall I make some coffee?' she countered, stalling for time as she made her way through to the kitchen. Nothing less than a complete account of the evening would satisfy her mother, and she didn't relish seeing Grace's air of expectant hope diminish to resigned disappointment.

'Well, did you?'

Karen filled the electric kettle and took down cups and saucers from the cupboard. 'It was quite enjoyable,' she answered warily, spooning instant coffee and sugar into two cups. As soon as the water boiled she poured it in and added milk.

'You didn't meet anyone?'

'That's a loaded question, Mother,' she protested with a faint trace of mockery. 'I met several people— about forty in all, and it was a perfectly splendid party. An abundance of good food and wine, and an array of guests that must have numbered highly among Auckland's social élite. Most of the women were attired according to the latest decree in fashion, and the men,' she paused fractionally before continuing on a note of cynicism, 'were impeccably groomed and the epitome of sophistication.'

Grace Ingalls' face mirrored her disappointment. 'There was no one——' she questioned faintly, and Karen stifled a feeling of remorse.

'I danced several times with different men,' she enlightened gently. 'All of whom were very charming.' Except one, she amended silently.

'Well, it's a start,' Grace conceded. 'No doubt you'll be invited again, and who knows?' she queried lightly.

Heaven forbid, Karen groaned, loath to parry any further innuendoes regarding her widowed state. The only way to foil her mother was to agree. 'Yes,' she answered blandly. 'Who knows? Did Lisa stir at all?' she asked in an attempt to change the subject.

'I didn't hear a sound,' Grace advised, and Karen pondered thoughtfully,

'Shall we take Lisa to the Parakai thermal pool at Helensville tomorrow? We can pack a picnic lunch, and aim to return home about three in the afternoon. I know you'll want to leave before tea so that you can arrive in Whangarei before dark.'

It was only when Karen crept between the sheets a short while later that she allowed herself to dwell on the evening's events—and the exasperating Matt Lucas. Something about him made her feel afraid—although why, she couldn't fathom.

Sunday brought sunshine, its gentle warmth encouraging those who basked beneath its rays to discard cardigans and seek a tan. There was scarcely a ripple of a breeze, and Karen packed the picnic hamper with a large bacon and egg pie she'd made the previous morning, together with buttered bread and a selection of fresh fruit. There was an iced chocolate cake, a flask of coffee, and orange cordial for Lisa.

The hour's drive, travelling first through the city and then heading in a north-westerly direction, seemed to pass swiftly, filled as it was with Lisa's inconsequential chatter. The little girl's excitement was evident, and Karen couldn't help giving a smile of maternal indulgence.

'Gran, look at me—look at me!' the little imp called from the shallow end of the heated pool, and Grace obligingly gave her granddaughter all her attention.

Karen watched with fierce pride as her daughter slowly swam towards her. 'That was very good, honey —really,' she complimented warmly, hugging the little girl close. 'Shall we get out now? I'm sure Gran is dying for some coffee. There'll be time for another swim after lunch.' She gave a conspiratorial wink. 'Race you to the side—away you go!'

Lisa scrambled out of the pool a few inches ahead of Karen. 'I won—I won!' she cried with delight. 'Next time you can win, Mummy, 'cos we'll start even.'

Karen laughed and scooped up a towel to place around her daughter's shoulders. 'Okay, that's a deal.' She dried the little girl off and helped her into a towelling robe, then followed suit. Her long hair streamed wetly down her back, but it would soon dry in the sun. After a long wet winter it felt good to laze idly beneath the warm rays as they caressed her limbs. With luck her skin would lose its paleness and tinge a light golden brown.

All too swiftly it was time for them to leave, and once home Grace immediately took her overnight bag from the bedroom she'd occupied during the weekend and placed it in the rear of her Mini.

'I'll arrange a small dinner party the next time you come home,' Grace confided to Karen as she slipped in behind the wheel.

Karen's heart immediately sank. She'd long ago given up discouraging her mother, for all it did was hurt her feelings, and she'd lost count of the number of times she'd endeavoured to explain that she neither felt lost nor alone. Each time she went home to Whangarei—which was regularly—Grace invariably managed to organise her numerous friends into providing a single eligible male among the guests. Carefully camouflaged as a small dinner party, or an extra ticket available for the cinema, it didn't fool Karen in the slightest, and she doubted it fooled anyone else.

"Bye, darling. Take care,' Grace bade through the open window of her car. 'I'll be back next Sunday. I hope around noon.'

Lisa followed the car to the gate and waved until the Mini moved out of sight, then she skipped across the thick green grass to stand at her mother's side.

'Are you going to weed the garden, Mummy, or are you going to mow the lawn?'

Karen leaned down and gave her an affectionate hug. 'Attack the weeds, I think. That should see us through until dinner. And speaking of dinner,' she chuckled engagingly, 'how do homemade hamburgers and chips sound— eaten in front of the television?'

'Lovely! Can we really?'

'I don't see why not,' she grinned down at the blonde imp bobbing up and down at her side. 'Now, weeds, here we come!'

There was something immensely satisfying about tending the earth, for free of restricting weeds the plants seemed almost to stretch and grow a little. Already the first signs of spring were in evidence, with new buds beginning to blossom on the peach trees in pink profusion. The vegetable garden showed a heartening growth of tender young plants that had been transplanted only the week before.

'Phew! I think that's enough for today,' Karen declared, wiping the dampness from her brow. 'Hop inside and run your bath, there's a good girl, while I put the lawnmower away. As soon as I've showered, I'll start making the hamburgers and chips.'

'Will we be in time to watch *Disneyland* on television?'

'If we hurry,' Karen assured her daughter, sparing a glance at her watch. She felt pleasantly tired, and looked forward to an early night in bed with a good book.

It was after ten o'clock when she switched off her bedside lamp and settled down beneath the covers. As always, sleep was elusive, and events of the past crowded forth from the deep recess they'd occupied during the light of day.

The dark hours—how she hated them. Even now, after nearly six years, memories invaded her sleep, bringing nightmares from which she would frequently wake bathed in sweat. Admittedly they occurred less often, but they were nonetheless hauntingly vivid.

Without conscious thought, Brad's face swam before her eyes, smiling at first, then becoming darkly sinister. She had been nineteen when he swept into her young life, a laughing attractive man with whom she had fallen swiftly in love. Despite advice to the contrary, she'd agreed to marry him almost at once, and their wedding had taken place a mere six weeks after their first meeting.

How rosy their future had seemed on that ill-fated day, and little did she suspect during the drive south from Whangarei that within a few hours her dreams would lie shattered beyond recall. They'd stopped at Warkworth for the night, a small town some thirty miles north of Auckland, and after signing the register Brad had preceded her to their room.

Expecting a loving, passionate husband, Karen was ill prepared for the change in his manner, for gone was the warm look of adoration, and in its place was an expression of smouldering hatred. In numb horror she'd watched as he locked the door, then he cruelly began to enlighten her as to precisely why he'd chosen her—not out of love, but revenge. By misfortune,

Karen bore a close physical resemblance to the girl who had jilted him quite literally at the altar more than a year ago, and it had been for revenge alone that he had sought Karen out.

What followed remained indelibly imprinted in her mind. At some stage of the night she must have fainted, for when she woke it was to find he had gone. She'd showered and dressed then, and had been on the point of leaving when she was confronted by a grave-faced policeman in the company of the hotel manager. Ironically, the news he imparted brought relief, not sorrow. Brad's car had been found at the bottom of a gorge several miles south of Auckland in the early hours of the morning, and he'd failed to survive the accident.

The sympathy from well-meaning friends was perhaps the worst thing Karen had to bear, and the need to get right away from the bittersweet memories Whangarei retained became imperative. Auckland, New Zealand's largest city, seemed the logical place to escape to, for it was just over a hundred miles south and was close enough to return home for a weekend whenever she chose.

Within a month she'd settled into an apartment and had a well-paid job as a typist for an accounting firm. Life began to assume something akin to normalcy again, only to be abruptly shattered by the discovery that she was pregnant. At first she was resentful, unwilling to accept a child as the living reminder of someone she wanted quite desperately to forget.

Lisa's entry into the world was premature and fraught with complications, and for days her tiny life hung in the balance. Like a beautiful flaxen-haired doll she lay in an incubator for more than a week, and it was a month before Karen could bring her home, looking so tiny and fragile, but with a healthy appetite and a strong pair of lungs.

With the need to provide security for her daughter, she'd decided to utilise a generous bequest from her paternal grandfather, purchasing after considerable deliberation a well-preserved wooden villa in suburban Remuera, less than eight miles from the inner city. Peaceful and secluded in a long, tree-lined street, the grounds were reasonably spacious with well-established trees and shrubs.

In the years that followed nothing untoward happened to mar their lives, and not once did Karen hanker for a social existence. Her mistrust of men remained deep-rooted, and she was totally unconcerned that she had earned the reputation of being ice-cold among the men of her acquaintance.

Soon after Lisa began primary school Karen found the days were dragging interminably long, and the need to occupy her time rather than financial necessity forced her to scan the 'situations vacant' column in the daily newspaper. One had leapt from the page as being ideal, and with previous secretarial experience she'd had no difficulty in securing it. Four hours each morning from nine until one o'clock suited her admirably, for it enabled her to drop Lisa at school en route to Newmarket, the inner-city suburb where Consolidated Electronics was situated. It had taken a few weeks to adjust, but after a month and a half Karen found a measure of satisfaction at being behind an office desk again.

Now, the absent, hitherto-mythical head of the firm was due to return the next day, and on the edge of sleep Karen stifled a slight smile. It would be interesting to witness Matt Lucas' expression when he discovered the girl he'd singled out for attention was in his employ.

CHAPTER TWO

'So much for spring sunshine!' Karen muttered beneath her breath as she parked her rain-splattered Datsun in an allotted space on the apron of bitumen immediately adjoining the double-storied concrete and steel complex that comprised the large electronics manufacturing firm.

At this time of year the weather tended to be contrary, and today was no exception. The wind that whipped her skirt held a chill that was the complete antithesis of the previous day.

The morning progressed without incident, and Karen began to relax slightly. It was ridiculous to feel edgy, but somehow she couldn't help it. Possibly Matt Lucas wouldn't discover her presence for several days, and even then he was unlikely to display any further interest. She liked her job, and didn't relish leaving to find another position—but she would if she had to.

'Good morning, beautiful. How was your weekend?'

Karen glanced up from the typewriter to meet Mike Evans' calculating gaze, and managed a polite smile. 'Fine, thank you.'

His darkly-handsome features assumed a wolfish grin. 'Only fine? You should have come out with me. I'd have given you something you wouldn't easily forget.'

He had such a high opinion of himself, it was unbelievable, she thought wryly. 'I'm busy,' she offered coolly, returning her attention to the work on hand, ignoring him completely as she set the necessary tabulations required for typing a complicated schedule.

'You're always busy,' he drawled. 'I declare you must be the most dedicated, efficient typist on record.'

'Because I remain indifferent to you?' she couldn't help parrying, and heard his soft chuckle.

'Come out with me tonight?'

'You know the answer to that.'

'Eventually you must change your mind,' Mike declared with the ease of self-assurance as he leaned against the edge of her desk.

Karen spared him a chilling glance as she carefully wound paper and carbon into the typewriter. 'That's most unlikely. If you don't mind, I have to get on with this.'

He didn't budge, and she was about to utter a scathing comment when the inter-office communication system on her desk gave forth a peremptory bleep. Reaching out, she depressed the appropriate button and murmured her name.

'Mrs Ingalls—Pamela Anderson, Mr Lucas' secretary,' a cool voice announced. 'Will you come upstairs to the Director's office? Turn right at the head of the stairs—its the suite at the end of the corridor.'

'Now?' Karen asked, momentarily nonplussed.

'Yes.' The line went dead, giving her little opportunity to demur.

'A summons from the almighty Matthew J. himself,' Mike pondered with interest. 'What have you been up to, Karen?'

'Perhaps he just wants to say "hello"?' she hazarded calmly, getting to her feet.

'Watch him, honey,' he cautioned with a knowing wink. 'He eats little girls for breakfast.'

Karen's disinterest wasn't feigned. 'Really?' She moved past him and made her way through the main office towards the foyer.

Upstairs, she was ushered into a luxuriously-fitted office, then the door closed behind her with a soft decisive snap.

Behind a large desk, his features an enigmatic mask, stood Matt Lucas, his tall frame outlined with startling clarity against the light streaming into the room from an expanse of plate-glass.

His dark blond hair was well-groomed, and a conservative business suit did little to tame the raw masculinity he emanated. Evident was a certain aura of power that was intimidating, and Karen wished the interview over and done with so that she could seek an escape from this disturbing man.

With alarming clarity she saw the tawny-gold eyes rake her slender frame with a lazy indolence that made her want to squirm beneath his gaze as she experienced a sensation not unlike that of a butterfly being pinned to the wall. Then slowly his features relaxed into a slight musing smile.

'The long arm of fate, wouldn't you agree?' Matt Lucas queried with cynical amusement. He waved a hand towards a few strategically-placed chairs. 'Do sit down.'

Karen mustered her composure, and with every evidence of calm she moved across the room and selected the chair furthest away from his desk. He, darn him, remained standing, and his height appeared formidable from where she sat.

With negligent ease he picked up a folder from his

desk and scanned its contents with seeming intentness. 'You've been with the firm for six weeks, I see,' he drawled, and she gave a brief monosyllabic affirmative.

'My Personnel Manager tells me you're punctual and proficient,' he continued leisurely, and she remained silent, wondering when he would come to the reason she'd been summoned here.

'Tell me, how long have you been widowed?'

The question caught her by surprise. 'I hadn't realised that was required personnel information,' she countered politely, meeting his steady gaze unflinchingly.

'I see from this——' he indicated the folder in his hand—'that you have a daughter aged five.'

'Yes.' What was this—some sort of inquisition?

'It's some years since you were last employed, I believe?'

Resentment began to flare, and she managed to control it with difficulty. He held the advantage by virtue of being her employer, but she was darned if she was going to tolerate any further questions regarding her personal life.

'Is the purpose of this interview to reprimand me in any way, Mr Lucas?' she queried bluntly. 'I'm due to leave at one, and I should complete typing the monthly schedule before I go.'

Matt Lucas' lips twisted into a slight smile. 'No,' he conceded, deliberately letting his gaze rove slowly over her attractively-attired form, approving the fashionable skirt and waistcoat in camel suede, the long-sleeved cream silk blouse, and the elegant high-heeled boots in matching camel suede. 'I was intrigued to discover whether the Karen Ingalls in my employ,' he continued softly, 'and the beautiful but rather—

hostile young woman I met the other night were one and the same.'

'And now that you have?' she queried repressively.

His eyes never left hers for a second, and she felt as if they stripped her soul. 'I'd like to endorse my invitation to dine.'

Slowly she rose to her feet as she fought for some measure of control. 'Does my job hinge on whether or not I accept?' Her eyes revealed some of the anger she was feeling. 'Because if it does, I'd like to tender my resignation.'

One eyebrow rose in quizzical amusement. 'Are you usually so antagonistic with members of the opposite sex?'

After a lengthy silence she offered steadily, 'I lead a socially inactive existence from choice, Mr Lucas. Last Saturday evening was an exception I've no intention of repeating.'

A slight smile curved the edges of his firm mouth. 'Your maternal devotion is admirable,' he commented silkily. 'However, I fail to see how a dinner engagement will endanger it.'

Karen maintained a tight rein on her temper. 'I'm sure there's a string of willing women among your acquaintance who'd delight in being selected to share your table. Why not ask one of them?'

'I prefer to ask you,' he inclined with lazy mockery.

'Thank you, Mr Lucas, but—no, thanks,' she refused.

'What if I insist?' he pursued softly.

The buzz of the telephone demanded his attention, and ignoring his directive to wait, she turned and quickly left the room.

By the time she reached the downstairs foyer she was visibly shaking, and she paused there for several seconds endeavouring to muster a calm composure before entering the main office.

It was an effort to resume typing, and it was only by concentrated willpower that she managed to complete the schedule with the minimum of errors.

For the first time she experienced a feeling of relief at leaving the building, and it wasn't until she was several miles distant that she began to relax. Bringing the car to a halt near the shopping centre in Remuera, she paused long enough to drink a hurried cup of coffee in a nearby coffee bar before collecting a few items of shopping, then she drove on to pick Lisa up from school.

'Did you have a nice day?' Karen asked warmly as minutes later the little blonde tot slipped into the front seat of the car.

'Hmm, lovely,' Lisa enthused. 'I got a stamp from the dental nurse, and another one from my teacher. The guineapigs have new babies, and Jeremy wants me to go to his party. I've got an invitation card in my schoolbag,' she added earnestly. 'Can I go?'

Karen laughed—a light bubbly sound that subsided into a chuckle of amusement. 'I don't think I could bear to live with myself if I said no. When is it to be?'

'Saturday, after lunch.'

Karen switched on the ignition and eased the car out from its parking space. 'Well, infant, we'd best hurry home. It's the afternoon for your ballet class.'

'I know,' Lisa grinned infectiously. 'Katherine said last week that I must practise, and I have, haven't I?'

Karen nodded a trifle absently as she concentrated

on the traffic ahead, and she listened with affection to her daughter's non-stop chatter during the short drive home.

The following day proved hectic, for one of the typists reported in sick, and Karen found herself having to cope with an extra workload. Consequently the morning flew more swiftly than usual, and the bleep of the intercom on her desk caused a frown of annoyance as she paused to answer it.

'Telephone, Karen,' the receptionist's voice announced. 'Take it on extension three.'

Anxiety furrowed her brow as she crossed to take the call. There were only two people who had this number —her mother, and the principal of Lisa's school. Lifting the receiver, she waited with bated breath for the caller to identify himself.

'Karen? Matt Lucas,' a deep voice drawled. 'Meet me in the downstairs foyer at once. I'll take you to lunch.'

Of all the nerve! 'I can't,' she refused flatly, as a mixture of relief and anger coursed through her veins.

'You're angry,' he voiced quietly. 'Why?'

'I don't take personal calls during working hours,' Karen said repressively.

'You expected an emergency,' Matt Lucas deduced thoughtfully. 'I'm sorry.'

She didn't say anything for a few seconds. 'I'm extremely busy. I'll have to go.'

'One o'clock, Karen.'

'I have to collect my daughter from school——'

'You'll get there on time. I have a two o'clock appointment.'

The click of the receiver being replaced left her

fuming with indignation. Just who did he think he was, for heaven's sake? He might have some jurisdiction over her working hours, but there was no way he was taking her for granted on her own time! At one o'clock he could wait in vain, for she would be gone.

She almost made it—almost. but not quite. Stepping through the foyer, she hurried towards the wide glass doors, only to come to an abrupt halt as she glimpsed Matt Lucas' tall frame leaning against a car parked directly in front of the main entrance.

'Taking flight? Shame on you, Karen,' Matt Lucas mocked quietly as she drew abreast.

'I'm on my own time, Mr Lucas,' she declared civilly. 'I've no desire to become a victim of office conjecture merely for the sake of your amusement.'

'Shall we go to lunch?' he suggested sardonically. 'Some food might improve your disposition.'

'I don't want to have lunch with you,' Karen exclaimed angrily.

'You need to eat,' he countered smoothly, looking down at her with a bland expression. 'Shall we go, or do you want to waste more time by arguing?'

He was impossible! 'Do you usually employ such steamrolling tactics?' she queried tartly, and saw him smile.

'I imagine you're quite unsquashable. In any case, to cause those delectable curves to be injured in such a manner would be a terrible waste. Now, shall we go?' He opened the passenger door of the gleaming cream XJ-S Jaguar, and with some misgivings Karen slipped into the front seat.

He slid in behind the wheel and set the car in motion. 'Do you like Italian food?'

'Would it matter if I didn't?'

'I've had a difficult morning,' Matt divulged patiently. 'I'd prefer to dine in amiable company.'

'Then perhaps you should eat alone,' she retorted. 'I didn't angle a luncheon date with you, and I'm here very much under protest.'

'Anyone would think I was intent on abducting you for an entirely salacious purpose,' he slanted musingly, 'when all I have in mind is the sharing of a pleasant meal.'

They were heading down towards Parnell, and there was a steady stream of traffic travelling in both directions. The sun was high, its warmth penetrating the tinted glass windscreen, and Karen couldn't help being aware of the car's luxurious interior—or, much to her chagrin, the man driving it.

'I don't know why you're doing this——'

'Don't you?' Matt mocked cynically. 'I thought it was obvious.'

'Just as obvious as my refusal must be to want any part of it,' she countered bitterly.

'What's so wrong in me wanting to get to know you better?'

'With what purpose in mind, Mr Lucas?' she queried with marked acerbity. 'A quick bedroom romp?'

His silence was enervating, and she began to feel unaccountably ashamed of her outburst.

'I'm almost tempted to bring the car to a halt and give you a taste of what you're so eager to accuse me of,' he evinced grimly, and when seconds later the car did slow down and slip into a parking space in Parnell Village, she felt a sense of fear.

'I'll catch a taxi back to Newmarket,' Karen indicated stoically, and deliberately focused her attention on the picturesque buildings lining the main street. Spanning several hundred yards, the numerous turn-of-the-century houses had been converted into shops and boutiques which offered a varied assortment of merchandise. The clothing boutiques were ultra-chic, and there was an atmosphere which couldn't be found anywhere else in Auckland.

'You'll do nothing of the kind,' Matt declared with exasperation. 'We'll eat lunch, then we'll return together.'

It wasn't a particularly enjoyable meal, conversation-wise, although the food was excellent, and Karen's appetite was negligible, so that she picked at the contents on her plate. When coffee appeared she gave an inaudible sigh of relief.

Five minutes later they were walking along the narrow alleyway towards the main street, and intent on keeping as much distance as possible between them, she missed an uneven patch in the brick-paved lane. The fine heel of her shoe caught the edge, making her stumble, and she would have fallen had Matt not reached out and grasped hold of her.

'Are you all right? Your ankle—you haven't twisted it?'

'No—no, I'm fine,' she assured him quickly, feeling suddenly breathless at his nearness.

'Do you think you can walk to the car?'

'What would you propose if I couldn't?' the words were out before she could give them a second thought, and his eyes gleamed with wicked humour.

'Why, carry you, Karen,' he drawled, and there was little she could do to hide the shocked expression that sprang into her eyes.

'I wouldn't allow you to,' she said quietly, and he smiled.

'Do you think you could stop me?'

She didn't say a word—anything at all would have seemed superfluous, and she accepted his casually-placed arm around her waist until they reached the car.

The drive back to Newmarket was achieved in silence, and Karen heaved a silent sigh of relief when they reached the parking area adjoining the large concrete and glass edifice that housed Consolidated Electronics. Good manners insisted she thank him, and she proffered the necessary words with polite detachment.

'Will you have dinner with me tomorrow evening?' Matt asked steadily, making no move to get out of the car. 'Nothing formal—just a quiet meal at my home.'

'No—I'm sorry, but I can't.'

He swung round in his seat and regarded her thoughtfully. 'The invitation is meant to include your daughter.'

Karen's face creased in an expression of disbelief. 'Lisa?'

'Why not?'

She glimpsed the slight mockery evident in his glance, but overriding it there was a calm determination she found difficult to comprehend. 'Thank you, but I must refuse.'

Matt spared a glance in the direction of his office. 'I can see my secretary making frantic signals from the window,' he declared, and sliding out from behind the wheel he moved round to open her door.

Karen slipped out, and made to turn in the direction of her own car, only to halt at the touch of his hand on her arm.

'Six-thirty tomorrow evening, Karen. I'll call for you.'

'You don't know where I live.'

A slight mocking smile teased the edges of his mouth. 'Your address is on file.'

'No. I——'

Whatever else she had been about to say was effectively stilled as his mouth covered hers in a brief hard kiss.

'How dare you!' she burst out in a furious undertone the instant he released her. 'What sort of conjecture do you imagine your secretary will put on that?' Her voice rose a fraction. 'I won't be known as your latest—fancy!'

'Ah, Karen, I do fancy you,' he murmured gently, and there were angry tears in her eyes as she shook her head at him vigorously.

'I won't have dinner with you, so don't bother calling for me.'

'Yes, you will,' he directed softly. 'Lisa will enjoy herself—even if her mother does not.' He straightened and allowed her to move away, then with a mocking salute he turned and disappeared into the building.

He was the very limit, she vowed wrathfully as she eased her Datsun out of its parking space. A thoroughly tantalising man—arrogant, self-assured, and incredibly bossy, she added for good measure. Altogether someone she should endeavour to avoid—although working for him didn't help matters at all. Perhaps it would be best if she *did* have dinner with him, for if she presented an ice-cool façade, he might give up and leave her alone. She'd been successful up until now at keeping the few men of her acquaintance at bay. Surely Matt Lucas wouldn't present too much of a problem.

However, as six-thirty the following evening drew near Karen wasn't so sure. Her stomach was behaving in a decidedly nervous fashion. If she could, she would have pleaded a headache and declined to go.

She eyed her reflection in the mirror and decided that the cream shirtwaster dress made her look too pale. Hurriedly she slipped it off and extracted a skirt and blouson-styled top of *challis* material, its honey and gold tonings on a black background accented her slight tan and highlighted her blonde hair to perfection. She smoothed a hand over its length and decided to leave it loose, rather than catch it into its customary knot at her nape.

'Mummy, there's a super car coming down our driveway. Is it *him*?'

Who else? Karen grimaced silently, and felt the butterflies in her stomach turn an abrupt somersault. Oh God, if only the evening could be over and done with. She'd no wish to go at all! With a sigh that defied description, she collected her shoulder-bag from the bed and moved down the hallway towards the front door. Lisa, with typical childish curiosity was already there, hopping up and down as she waited for the door to be opened.

Karen's greeting was coolly polite, and because of Lisa's presence she forced a smile to her lips. 'Won't you come in?'

Matt's eyes held a gleam of admiration as they roved appreciatively over her slender form, then his gaze shifted to the doll-like figure at her side. 'Hello,

Lisa,' he said quietly, and was immediately rewarded by a shy smile. 'If you're both ready, we'll go.'

All Karen's instincts screamed out for her to refuse, and Matt seemed to sense it, for he calmly reached out and caught hold of her arm. Nothing short of a struggle would have permitted her escape, and she found herself closing the door and walking quietly by his side to the car.

The drive wasn't a long one, a mere ten minutes along the main thoroughfare that led towards the waterfront. Quite what she expected of his home she was not sure, but, nothing prepared her for the gracious double-storied mansion set in tree-studded grounds totally secluded from the road. On the rise above Kohimarama beach, the house was constructed of a pleasing mixture of brick and timber. Sparkling white-painted wood contrasted vividly with the dark rough-cast brick base, and multi-paned windows flanked by dark blue shutters gave an overall colonial appearance.

'Do you live here all by yourself?' Lisa queried incredulously as the car crunched to a halt outside the main entrance, and Matt laughed.

'Not quite. A very capable housekeeper cooks my meals and looks after the house. Her husband does the garden, lawns, and sees to general maintenance. You'll meet them in a few minutes.'

The house was just as impressive inside as it was out, and Karen endeavoured to hide her admiration as her gaze wandered from the lush deep-piled camel-toned carpet to the expensive prints gracing the walls of the impressive foyer.

A well-proportioned woman of middle years hovered

in the foreground, a welcoming smile creasing her pleasant features.

'Mrs Rogers—Karen Ingalls, and this young lady is her daughter Lisa,' Matt introduced with ease.

'What a dear wee mite,' the housekeeper responded warmly, and Matt's answering smile held indulgence. 'Dinner will be ready at seven,' she said, adding, 'I'll be in the kitchen if you need me.' With a smile she turned and disappeared through a door leading off to the left.

'Come into the lounge,' Matt directed smoothly, and Karen clutched Lisa's hand more tightly within her own as she followed him into a spacious, superbly-furnished room. Muted shades of beige were reflected in the textured fabric covering the walls, and the drapes at the windows were of velvet in a soft shade of sage-green, as were the many sofas and chairs. Mahogany furniture complemented the colour scheme, and the total effect was one of tasteful elegance.

'Can I get you something to drink?'

Karen glanced across the space between them and gave an imperceptible murmur of assent. Heaven knew she needed something to calm her rapidly accelerating nerves!

'Spirits?' Matt queried idly, crossing to a well-stocked liquor cabinet. 'Or something light—a medium sherry, perhaps?'

'Sherry will be fine,' she managed evenly.

'Some lemonade, Lisa?'

'Yes, please,' that infant responded with an alacrity that brought a slight frown to her mother's brow and a smile to her host's lips.

Skilfully Matt engaged the little girl in conversation, listening with what appeared to be genuine interest

as she answered his questions about school. He seemed
to inspire confidence, and Karen had to hide her surprise. Lisa was usually shy in the presence of strangers,
but with Matt Lucas she was responding as if he was
someone she'd known all her young life.

Dinner was an excellent meal comprising three
courses, and designed, Karen suspected, to cater to
a young child's taste. There was chicken consommé,
followed by filet mignon, with creamed potatoes,
green peas, carrots, and zucinni in a delicate sauce,
with a compote of fresh fruit served with cream for
dessert. Accompanied by a delicate wine, a rosé of
Australian vintage that was an excellent complement,
and of which much to Lisa's delight she was permitted
a small quantity in a glass of her own, they sat back
over an hour later feeling fully replete.

'We'll have coffee in the lounge,' Matt indicated
with a smile as they left the table, and Karen cast a
hurried glance at her watch.

'We must leave soon,' she excused, conscious of the
look of disappointment that appeared on her daughter's face. 'Lisa has school tomorrow.'

'Oh, Mummy, it's early yet!'

'Nevertheless, we can't stay late,' Karen stated
firmly, meeting Matt's thoughtful gaze.

'I think we should make plans for an evening when
there's no school the following day,' he suggested,
and at once the little girl's face broke into a wide
smile.

'Lovely—can it be this Friday? I'm going to a birthday party on Saturday, and my Gran's taking me to
Whangarei for the school holidays on Sunday.'

'Lisa!' Karen's reprimand was rather more sharp

than was warranted, and Lisa shot her mother a faintly puzzled look.

'Friday will be fine,' Matt agreed gently. 'I'll arrange a time with your mother.'

'You're nice.' Lisa looked up into the tawny eyes far above her own, and declared earnestly, 'I like you.'

His lips parted and moved to form a crooked smile. 'I like you, too, infant.'

Karen felt unaccountably angry, and the look she flashed Matt spoke volumes. In fact, it was a wonder he didn't reel from the attack!

'I'll forgo coffee, if you don't mind,' she said with a wintry smile, adding with determination, 'I'll take Lisa out to the car.'

Karen didn't say a word on the way home, and the minute they halted in the driveway outside her home she slid from the car, bundling Lisa out with as much speed as possible. Her thanks were a bare facsimile and in no way resembled the intended meaning of that simply-voiced platitude. She didn't even look back as she inserted the key into the front door, and when she turned round to close it, the Jaguar's tail-lights were a rapidly-disappearing twin blaze of red.

Karen spent the entire four hours of the following morning in a state of trepidation. Twice she considered confronting the Personnel Manager with her resignation, for to continue working for Matt Lucas was unthinkable. It was fortunate that she didn't depend on a salary for Lisa's and her own support. What remained of her grandfather's bequest had been carefully invested to provide a comfortable income.

Dammit, she cursed silently. Where was Brian Winters, the Personnel Manager? He'd spent the first half of the morning in conference, and now it appeared he'd left the office for an appointment elsewhere. She spared her watch a hurried glance, and determined she had less than ten minutes until she left for the day. There was nothing else for it but to put her resignation in writing.

Suiting thoughts to action, she inserted a sheet of paper into her typewriter, tapped out the few words necessary, then withdrew it and attached her name with an angry flourish.

'Well, well,' a familiar voice drawled. 'And how are you this morning?'

Karen looked up and encountered Mike Evans' sardonic expression. 'Fine, and you?' she responded evenly, returning her attention to the paper she'd just signed. She folded it into an envelope, which she sealed and addressed.

'So you've decided to by-pass the lower echelon and make a play for the top brass, hmm?'

She gave a slightly puzzled frown. 'You're talking in riddles.'

'I'll refresh your memory,' he declared laconically. 'Yesterday you left with our eminent Director, and returned almost an hour later. Fast work, Karen,' he accorded softly. 'Was it lunch—or didn't you bother with *food*?'

'Your mind needs fumigating!' she snapped, shooting him a venomous glare as she stood to her feet. 'If you'll excuse me, I'll deliver this, then go to lunch.' She went to move past him and felt him grip her arm.

'My, my—maybe there's fire beneath the ice, after all.'

Karen deliberately let her eyes sweep down to his hand on her arm, then back again, and he laughed.

'Is he as good in the sack as they say?'

'Haven't you something to do—like returning to the factory, where you should be?'

'Yes,' a deep voice concurred silkily, 'an excellent suggestion, Evans, wouldn't you say?'

Karen swung round and came face-to-face with Matt, who was standing with apparent indolence less than a yard distant. In that instant Mike Evans gave a negligent shrug and turned away, and with a wrathful glare that was more eloquent than mere words could ever have been, she swept past them both.

By the time she reached the foyer she was trembling with anger, and incapable of uttering a word. An arm leant forward and pushed open the door, but she ignored the courtesy and all but ran down the steps towards her car.

She didn't see the XJ-S Jaguar parked beside her Datsun until it was too late, and suddenly Matt was there beside her, tall and frighteningly large at such close proximity.

He opened the door of his car and indicated the passenger seat. 'Get in, Karen.' It was a brusque command that boded ill for anyone with sufficient temerity to consider disregarding it.

'No,' she refused baldly.

'Don't argue.' His voice was ominously quiet, but she threw caution to the winds.

'I've no argument with you—in fact, I have nothing to say to you at all!'

'Has Mike Evans been bothering you?'

Anger erupted into indignant speech. '*You* bother me!' she cried furiously. 'What difference does it make? I wish you'd both leave me alone!'

'Is it marriage, or men in general?' Matt queried idly.

Karen felt as if she could hit him. 'You know nothing about my marriage—what's more, it's none of your business.'

'That remains to be seen,' he intoned obliquely. 'Let's go to lunch.'

'Oh—go to hell!'

Swift anger tautened his features, sending a shiver of apprehension down her spine. 'By the living heaven,' he breathed heavily, 'you believe in trying a man's patience to the very limit, don't you?'

She held his gaze steadily. 'I don't like men who try to win my daughter's affection in an effort to sway mine.'

His eyes narrowed slightly. 'You accuse me of doing that?'

'Aren't you?' she countered with intended sarcasm, then wavered somewhat beneath those penetrating tawny depths as they raked her features.

After a measurable silence, he stated deliberately, 'No.'

The anger drained away, leaving her pale. 'You may as well know I'm leaving the firm.' She offered him the envelope she still held in her hand. 'You can have this—it's my resignation.'

He took it and slid it into the pocket of his jacket. 'That was inevitable,' he considered, his expression deliberately enigmatic. 'Effective from when?'

'Friday of next week,' she returned resolutely.

Matt continued to regard her thoughtfully. 'I've reserved a table for tomorrow evening. I'll call for you at six-thirty.'

Karen looked at him in disbelief. 'No, I——'

'Think how disappointed Lisa will be if you refuse to come,' he interrupted smoothly.

'You ride roughshod over everyone, don't you?' she accused in a furious undertone. 'Why can't you leave me alone? I like my life the way it is.'

'I'll see you tomorrow evening,' he declared dryly, ignoring her stormy features.

'You won't!'

Matt leaned out a negligent hand and touched her cheek, letting his fingers trail down to lift her chin. 'I seem to recall we've had this conversation before.' He bent down and brushed her lips lightly with his own, then he turned and moved round the car to slip in behind the wheel. His hand effected a mocking salute as he drove away.

Karen felt like screaming with frustrated anger, and for the remainder of the day she exerted as much physical energy as possible on household chores, falling into bed from near-exhaustion long after Lisa had settled down for the night.

CHAPTER THREE

QUITE what Karen expected at work the following morning she wasn't sure. Certainly she expected to be summoned by the Personnel Manager, but she wasn't prepared for the knowing glances in her direction from the other girls in the office.

Conversations had a habit of suddenly coming to a halt whenever she entered a room, and it made her feel faintly sick over the conjecture the clerical staff placed on her leaving.

Twice she was on the point of ringing through to Matt Lucas to cancel their date, and only the fact that her conversation would be overheard prevented her from making the call.

As the day progressed she became more wary, and Lisa's excited anticipation didn't help matters at all. She wished she'd never accepted the invitation—not that she'd had much choice. Damn Matt for issuing it in Lisa's presence, thus placing her in an awkward position.

A calf-length dress in sky-blue silk clung to her slender curves, its soft folds cunningly seamed in an unusual design that was startlingly elegant. Apart from highlighting her eyes with mascara and the careful application of eye-shadow, she wore the minimum of make-up, and her freshly-washed hair swung loose, bouncing almost as if it had a life of its own with every movement she made.

'You look really nice. You smell nice, too.' Lisa

wrinkled her nose, and Karen gave her an affectionate hug.

'You're looking forward to going out, aren't you?'

Lisa's face broke into an engaging grin, and her large hazel eyes positively sparkled. 'Oh yes! I haven't ever been to a resta——' she stumbled over the word, then tried again, 'restaurant—I got it right! Will there be lots of people there?'

'Quite a few, I expect,' Karen found herself answering distractedly, for Matt's car had just whispered to a halt in the driveway.

At the sound of a knock Lisa broke into a run in her hurry to get to the door, and Karen heard her excited voice mingling with a deep masculine drawl as she made her way down the hall.

'My, my,' Matt declared as she came into view. 'It's not often I get the opportunity to escort two attractive young women to dinner.' His eyes travelled over her slim figure with appreciative approval, and she willed herself not to blush.

She didn't like him, much less want to go out with him, so why she should be feeling like a teenager about to embark on her first date was beyond her comprehension.

He bore an air of assured sophistication, looking very much the successful businessman. His light grey suit was impeccably tailored, his shirt of cream silk and an elegantly-knotted tie a perfect complement.

For Lisa's sake Karen smiled a greeting and bade him enter. 'Would you care for a drink?'

Matt shook his head in dissent. 'If you're both ready, we'll get on our way.'

'Oh, good,' Lisa beamed. 'I like riding in your car.'

Matt laughed with genuine amusement, and caught

her hand in his. 'Come on then, infant. I can see I rate a deplorable third.'

'Second,' Lisa grinned, unabashed.

'What about dinner?' he mocked quizzically, and she gave a delicious chuckle.

'Well, I *am* hungry.'

'Lisa!' Karen protested, but it had little effect, and Matt merely walked on ahead to the car, leaving her to shut the door and follow.

Lisa was in her element, her eyes widening in wonderment at her first experience of dining out, and conscious of her daughter's avid interest in everything —Matt Lucas, especially—Karen was forced to place her mistrustful dislike to one side and make conversation. Although why, she wasn't sure, for Lisa seemed intent on filling her newly-acquired friend with as much information as she could find. Everything from their pet kitten to a loose tooth, Gran's frequent visits, her friends, the teacher at school, was aired, and once when Karen would have chastised her Matt broke in with a smiling dismissal, then he proceeded to ask questions which brought forth a positive flood of answers.

'You're going to a party tomorrow, I believe,' Matt smiled, and Lisa paused as she swallowed a mouthful of food.

'Yes. It's in the afternoon,' she imparted brightly. 'Jeremy's in my class.'

'Ah, Jeremy,' he nodded sagely, and she gave an engaging grin.

'I guess he likes me—he brings me candies and things.'

Matt broke into quiet laughter, his eyes crinkling with humour. 'I'd say Jeremy is a very smart young man.'

'He's good at writing and spelling, too,' Lisa said with utter seriousness. 'He gets a stamp from the teacher nearly every day.'

It was almost ten when they left, and Lisa, replete with good food and tired from all the excitement, promptly fell asleep with the motion of the car.

'I'll take her,' Matt indicated quietly as soon as the Jaguar drew to a halt outside her home, and Karen said stiffly,

'It's all right—I can manage.'

'In that case, give me the key and I'll unlock the front door.'

No, Karen wanted to cry out, I don't want you to come in. Aloud she said, 'I wouldn't think of delaying you, Mr Lucas. Thank you for an enjoyable evening.' She felt for the clasp and opened the door, slipping out to stand on the path, and she hadn't taken more than three steps when he fell into step beside her.

As they reached the porch, he silently extended his hand for the key, and the glance she flung him lost much of its venom in the darkness.

He walked in ahead of her and switched on the light, leaving her standing in the doorway in angry silence. For a moment she considered ordering him to leave, but the fact that Lisa might stir called for some restraint.

It took five minutes to undress and put the little girl to bed, and when Karen returned, Matt was standing in the lounge, hands thrust into his trouser pockets, his rugged features thoughtful.

Karen regarded him silently, her eyes faintly wary.

'I see several photographs displayed of Lisa, and one

of a couple I presume to be your parents,' he indicated quietly. 'But not even one that could be your late husband.'

She felt the breath catch in her throat, and she swallowed compulsively. 'I do have a marriage certificate,' she managed frigidly, and saw him grimace.

'It wasn't my intention to imply otherwise.'

'No?'

'I was merely curious as to why Lisa's father has no place among the family photographs. It would indicate he died when she was very young—even before she was born,' he ventured. 'Any mention of the word "Daddy" has been conspicuous by virtue of its absence in her conversation.'

A wild, uncontrollable anger was mounting inside Karen's breast, making her want to lash out at this indomitable man and his insidious comments. Her eyes sparkled with fury as she snapped, 'I don't owe you any explanation, and you've got a hell of a nerve coming in here, behaving like some—some lawyer for the prosecution!' She paused for breath, then went on in an odd little rush. 'Will you please leave?' Angry tears filled her eyes, and she blinked furiously to control their imminent flow.

Matt looked down at her, his expression unreadable, and after an interminable length of time Karen turned away.

She was making a complete fool of herself, she decided shakily. Surely she could have handled the situation with uncaring *sang-froid*, instead of falling apart at the seams.

A few seconds later Matt moved past her and left the room, closing the front door behind him with an almost silent click, then the Jaguar reversed down the drive, its engine an imperceptible whisper in the clear night air.

Jeremy Trenwith lived less than two miles away, and it was Karen's intention to drop Lisa off after she'd introduced herself, and return when the party was due to conclude. However, she was foiled in this attempt soon after Jeremy's mother came to the door with her son in tow.

'Hi, Lisa.'

'Hello, Jeremy.'

An ordinary enough greeting, but the manner in which it was spoken had each mother striving to conceal a smile.

'Do come in,' Karen was beguiled. 'I'm Janine,' the attractive brunette confided engagingly. 'You will stay, won't you?'

'Well, I——'

'Oh, do. Please,' the other beseeched with an unashamed grin. 'Mind you, it's only fair to warn that the invitation is double-edged.'

'Help?' Karen smiled, and Janine Trenwith broke into mirthful laughter.

'In capital letters! Will you?'

'I'd be delighted.'

Indoors there was mild chaos erupting from the lounge as what appeared at first sight to be a room filled with children fighting for supremacy and Jeremy's attention.

'We got a bit carried away with the invitations,' Janine explained with a captivating smile. 'Jeremy insisted it was all or nothing—hence the entire junior class. Jason, the cowardly man,' she wrinkled her nose expressively, 'has done a bunk, vowing to put in an appearance when my brother arrives—which,' she took time to spare her watch a glance, 'should be soon. Meanwhile, I think something in the way of a lolly scramble might quieten things down for a few minutes. Blast the rain,' she cursed inelegantly. 'I hadn't bargained on having indoor games.'

'If we put our heads together, I'm sure we can come up with something,' Karen began tentatively. 'Perhaps we could organise them into circles, ten in each, and have them pass an object around to music. Whoever has the object in his hand when the music stops is out. That should take ten minutes or so.'

'Why didn't I think of that? Come on, Karen—into battle!' the other girl declared with a rueful grin.

Thirty minutes later their faces were flushed with exertion. It seemed to amuse the children to have two grown-ups indulging in childish games, and they clamoured for Janine and Karen to be blindfolded for Blind Man's Buff. With a smile of resignation they allowed themselves to have a blindfold applied, and the game began.

'I wouldn't have believed it if I hadn't seen it with my own eyes,' a strange male voice commented with laughing indulgence, and Karen heard Janine pass up a fervent,

'Praise the lord—reinforcement has arrived!'

'From that, I gather our presence is welcome,' a familiar voice drawled, and Karen felt her heart jolt, then take on a faster beat.

Slowly she removed the blindfold, and her worst fears were confirmed as she came face-to-face with Matt Lucas. Her first instinct was to gather Lisa up in her arms and escape.

Janine began to perform the introductions, and when she came to her brother he smiled and gave a negligent wave of his hand.

'We've already met,' he interrupted with assumed indolence. 'Haven't we, Karen?' His eyes gleamed with hidden amusement as she murmured an assent.

'How nice,' his sister proclaimed happily. 'If it hadn't have been for Karen, I'd be a quivering wreck by now.' She aimed a playful punch at her husband's chest. 'You and Matt can take control for half an hour, while Karen and I quaff a much-needed cup of coffee, then we'll feed the masses.'

Two hours later the last of the children had been collected and taken home, and Karen dried the last remaining plate, then she replaced the tea-towel on the rack.

'It's been a very enjoyable party. Thank you for asking me to stay.' She gave Janine a smile and indicated, 'I'll just get Lisa——'

'You won't,' the other girl declared firmly. 'You're staying for dinner. You deserve to be fed after all the help you've given this afternoon.'

'I couldn't do that,' Karen protested.

'Is your husband expecting you home?'

'No,' she denied slowly.

'In that case, you've no reason to hurry away. Dinner is all ready—I prepared it this morning. It simply needs re-heating. Oh, heavens,' she exclaimed as the doorbell peeled. 'That will be Mother. Excuse me a moment while I let her in.'

This was turning out to be a family affair, of which Karen occupied no rightful part. She *couldn't* stay, not with Janine's hateful brother as a fellow guest.

When Janine came back she'd make some excuse and leave.

However, her efforts to withdraw were successfully forestalled by a totally irrepressible hostess, and Karen couldn't help thinking darkly that it was a trait Janine shared with her impossible brother.

She was drawn into the lounge for a pre-dinner drink, and there was no opportunity for her to avoid Matt as he crossed to her side, his eyebrows arched in silent quizzical query.

'Surprised to see me?'

Karen forced a slight smile to her lips. 'I couldn't be expected to know you would be here.'

'And if you had known, you wouldn't have come,' he drawled cynically.

'I brought Lisa to your nephew's birthday party,' she said quietly.

'Unaware that I was a part of the family,' he murmured musingly. 'It would appear we're to dine together again.'

'Unfortunately.'

'Ah, my dear Karen,' he drawled. 'I'm really quite good company.'

'I don't doubt you are,' she responded with intended sarcasm, and he laughed, the corners of his eyes creasing in amusement.

It was a relief when Janine announced dinner, and Karen found herself seated next to Matt, much to her chagrin, for his close proximity quite spoiled her appetite.

Lisa and Jeremy were seated together at the opposite end of the table, and they chattered incessantly all through the meal.

'Lisa is your replica in miniature,' Matt indicated softly as they moved from the table and made their way to the lounge.

Aware that others were within hearing distance, Karen merely smiled and moved away.

'My dear, how nice of you to stay and help Janine,' Mrs Lucas extolled warmly as she crossed to Karen's side. 'You also know Matt, I believe.'

Matt casually joined them, breaking in with sardonic cynicism, 'Pity the poor girl, Mother—she works for me.'

'Ah, I see.' Mrs Lucas' expression was revealing, and her son laughed. 'He's something of a tyrant,' she explained lightly, then added with an irresistible smile, 'Do you find him so?'

'Come, Karen,' he mocked. 'Nothing less than the truth will do.'

'As you said, I work for you,' Karen countered sweetly. 'And there are times when the necessity for tact overrules total honesty.'

'Oh, well done,' Mrs Lucas accorded as she directed Matt a mischievous twinkle.

'You never mentioned that you work for Matt,' Janine broke in with interest, and Karen endeavoured to meet the other girl's inquisitive gaze.

'I wasn't aware you and Matt were related,' she managed faintly.

'What a wonderful coincidence,' Janine enthused as she cast first Karen, then Matt, a speculative gleam. 'I couldn't have planned it better myself.'

'Matchmaking, my dear sister?' Matt mocked gently. 'I'm quite capable of managing my own affairs.'

'Oh, yes, we know,' his sister teased unmercifully. 'You've acquired quite a reputation in that direction.'

'I think it's going to be an early summer, don't you?'
Mrs Lucas interjected, directing the query towards
Karen and blandly ignoring her siblings' lighthearted
bantering.

Karen's slightly strangled affirmative brought forth
an understanding smile. 'I really should be leaving,'
she excused herself.

'Well, it's been very nice meeting you, my dear. I'm
sure we'll see each other again.'

With Lisa's hand firmly tucked in her own, they
made their farewells. It was a relief to get into the car,
although the faintly quizzical gleam Matt directed her
as she bade him a polite goodnight did nothing to help
her composure. She was darned if she would allow him
to have the upper hand, although instinct warned that
he was skilfully adept at handling women. After her
outburst last night, it was doubtful he would seek her
company again.

She told herself fiercely that she didn't want him to
—but an inner voice cried out to the contrary, and that
night she awoke in the early morning hours as a vivid
reminder of Brad returned in nightmare form to taunt
her.

Grace Ingalls returned at noon the following day, and
she hadn't been in the house ten minutes before Lisa
began regaling events of the past week.

'—and Wednesday night we went to Matt's place for
dinner, and Friday night he took Mummy and me to a
restaurant,' she completed triumphantly. 'Yesterday I
went to Jeremy's party, and guess what? Matt is
Jeremy's uncle.' The little girl turned towards Karen
and smiled, then swung back to face her grandmother.
'He has a lovely car, and an awfully big house. A lady

and her husband look after him, don't they, Mummy?'

'That sounds nice, darling,' Grace commented warmly. 'I'm glad you've been having such a lovely time. Now, why don't you go into your room and check you have everything you need to take away.'

Oh lord, Karen sighed inwardly. Now she would be bombarded with questions! Sure enough, they began the instant Lisa was out of earshot.

'Matt? Just who is this man, Karen? You didn't tell me you were going out with anyone.'

She answered them strictly in order. 'His name is Matt Lucas, and I work for him. I'm not going out with him in the way you mean. He issued the invitations more for Lisa's benefit than mine.'

'Lisa? Oh, come on, darling,' Grace laughed. 'He might have chosen to let you think that, but it's you that he's after.'

'He's not,' Karen denied emphatically. 'What's more, I don't imagine I'll see him again.'

'What about the party Lisa was talking about?'

'Neither of us realised the other would be there,' she explained patiently, hoping to throw her mother off the scent.

'But you said you work for him,' Grace exclaimed. 'Surely you'll see him there. What position does he have with the firm?'

This was getting worse by the minute! 'Director,' Karen admitted reluctantly.

'You mean he's head of the firm?' Grace couldn't hide her incredulity, nor her delight. 'Darling, you must——'

'What, Mother?' she queried cynically. 'Entice him into my lair?'

'Well,' Grace murmured deprecatorily, 'he appears to be a good catch, and——'

'I should have a husband, and Lisa should have a father,' Karen interrupted bitterly. 'I've heard all that before.'

'Not all men are like Brad,' Grace ventured cautiously.

'I'm not willing to take the risk of finding out,' Karen said with cold finality, and her mother uttered a heartfelt sigh.

'I hate to see you so bitter, Karen. I had hoped that——'

'After six years I'd be over it? That it could be all nicely parcelled away in some dark cupboard and conveniently forgotten?' she queried with unaccustomed cynicism.

Grace's expression became earnest. 'Surely——'

'I learnt my lesson the hard way, remember?' Karen mocked, and her mother ventured tentatively,

'You haven't told him anything?'

'Why rake over old ashes? I don't want any pity.'

Grace gave a sigh that behoved great forbearance. 'Substitute pity for understanding. He's entitled to know, don't you think?'

'Why?' Karen questioned baldly. 'You're talking as if the man has marriage in mind.' She laughed derisively. 'He has yet to proposition me, let alone propose!' She sobered quickly. 'Even if he did, I wouldn't accept.'

'I hate to think of you so alone,' her mother wailed. 'What will you do when Lisa grows up and leaves home?'

'Find some absorbing hobby to fill my daylight

hours,' Karen answered quickly, and Grace asked searchingly,

'What of all the empty, lonely nights?'

'This conversation has reached its limits,' Karen said steadily, giving her mother a particularly direct look. 'Shall we have lunch?'

It wasn't until later when Grace had left with Lisa that Karen allowed herself to reflect on her mother's maxim. Somehow the empty house seemed to echo those same words, making a mockery of her own emphatic avowal to the contrary.

Oh, what was the matter with her? She felt cross and out of sorts—almost as if she might be coming down with something. The 'flu, perhaps? But her throat wasn't sore, and her head didn't ache. It had to be Lisa's absence that was to blame, for this was the first time they'd spent several days apart since the little girl was born. Suddenly the week yawned ahead, and Friday, when she would drive north for the weekend, seemed a very long way away.

It didn't take a detective to discern why Karen was the recipient of several speculative glances when she entered the office next morning. It was patently obvious that the secretarial grapevine was responsible for relaying details regarding her encounter with Matt Lucas in the parking area—and she didn't doubt that the gossip had been embellished along the way.

The best thing was to ignore it, and she deliberately set herself the task of diminishing the pile of paperwork crowding the in-tray on her desk.

'So you're the latest,' a feminine voice drawled with unveiled sarcasm, and Karen looked up to encounter an icy glare directed down on her hitherto unsuspecting head.

Susan Browning, acting as secretary to both the Manager and the Accountant, stood poised to strike like an angry disgruntled snake defending its territory—and it didn't take much effort for Karen to work out that Susan considered their exalted Director her particular property.

'I beg your pardon?' Karen queried mildly in the hope of averting what looked like being a quarrel.

'Oh, come on—don't act the dumb blonde! This room has windows that command a splendid view of the adjacent parking area.'

'I'm aware of that,' she managed calmly, and the other girl gave a derisive snort.

'"Aware of that", are you?' Susan mimicked belligerently. 'I can't imagine what's come over Matt. He usually displays more finesse.' She went on cruelly, 'Obviously your—er—talents must be considerable.'

Karen just looked at her, unable to believe anyone could be capable of such invective. 'You're quite wrong,' she assured quietly.

'Oh, come on! Who do you think you're kidding?' A malevolent gleam entered the girl's eyes. 'A word of advice, dear—our ever-so-charming Director isn't exactly the faithful type. I wouldn't pin any hopes on holding his interest for very long.'

'Believe me, Susan,' Karen answered evenly, 'I wouldn't want to.' Quickly she gathered up her bag and slid the cover over the typewriter, then with a determined smile she turned and walked out of the office.

Stupid angry tears were beginning to burn the back of her eyes as she made her way into the foyer. First

Mike Evans, and now Susan. It was just too much! Thank heavens she was leaving on Friday, for that day couldn't come soon enough.

'Oh!' She gave a startled gasp as she collided with a solid frame, and her consternation increased when she discovered the steadying hand on her arm belonged to none other than Matt himself.

'Are you all right?'

Karen shied away from his intent scrutiny. 'Yes, I'm fine. In a hurry, though. I'm late for an appointment,' she invented wildly. She turned and almost ran towards the entrance doors in her anxiety to escape his presence, and only when her car was edging its way out of the parking area did she begin to relax.

The house seemed empty without Lisa's energetic presence, and the long hours ahead needed to be filled with some constructive task, otherwise she'd go mad! The sewing machine provided the answer, for she'd bought a few lengths of material only the week before with the intention of making two new sun-frocks for Lisa for the coming summer. That should take care of the afternoon very satisfactorily, then she'd prepare an easy meal and view television.

At six o'clock Karen lifted the sewing machine down and put it away in its cabinet, satisfied that only the hand-sewing remained to be done. She stretched her arms, easing the slight ache in her shoulders, then made her way into the kitchen.

Something light and easily prepared would do for her evening meal, and she took eggs and butter from the refrigerator. Scrambled eggs on toast, with some coffee, sounded fine, and she broke the eggs into a bowl, added a dash of milk and some herbs, then began beating the mixture with a fork.

An insistent staccato knock on the front door brought a momentary frown, for she wasn't expecting anyone to call. Setting the bowl down, she wiped her hands, and was almost to the door when the knocking was repeated.

Her fingers hovered near the knob as she queried cautiously, 'Who is it?'

'Matt Lucas.'

There was no doubting that deep voice, but still she hesitated, opening the door only a fraction. 'What do you want?'

'I won't be accused of forcing my way in, Karen,' Matt drawled.

Without a word she held the door open, feeling oddly intimidated as he moved into the wide hall to stand several feet distant, one hand thrust negligently into a trouser pocket as he surveyed her.

His silent appraisal was unnerving, and after several timeless seconds she said stiffly, 'I was in the kitchen fixing dinner. What do you——'

'Put it back in the refrigerator, Karen,' he directed sardonically. 'I'm taking you out.'

'You are not!' she spluttered indignantly. 'You can't arrive on my doorstep and order me about. Besides, I've already mixed the eggs——'

'They'll keep until breakfast,' Matt soothed, in a manner such as one would adopt to calm a fractious child. 'Go and change, fix your hair, and do whatever you consider essential to your face.'

'No!' Her eyes sparked alive with temper. 'This is my house, and you have no——' Her words were effectively stilled by his mouth on hers, and the gasp she uttered became trapped in her throat.

For a few heart-stopping seconds she was too surprised

to struggle, then reaction set in, and she lashed out with her fists, her feet—all to no avail, for he simply drew her close against his hard frame, sliding one hand behind her head to hold it firm, while the other arm curved down her back. She balled her hands into fists and beat against his back, her voice dulled into a furious moan as his mouth forced her lips apart, teasing gently with consummate skill until her struggles began to lessen, then his hands moved, caressing her back and shoulders in a manner that sent waves of warmth flooding her limbs.

His lips trailed down the sensitive pulsing cord to the base of her neck in a teasing, provocative manner that brought forth an unbidden gasp of pleasure before his mouth sought hers in a kiss that left her weak-limbed and oddly breathless.

At last, when she thought she could stand it no longer without responding, he drew back and put her at arm's length. A slight smile curved his lips as he looked down at her. 'Go and change,' he bade quietly.

Rather shakily Karen raised a hand to push back a few stray locks of hair that had fallen forward. 'If you think you've kissed me into submission, you're mistaken,' she managed evenly—a difficult feat when her heart was racing and her breathing seemed strangely affected.

'Have dinner with me, anyway,' Matt directed lazily.

'I was going to have an early night,' she protested, not at all sure it would be wise to accept.

'If I assure you that I merely want your company for dinner,' he began tolerantly, 'will that influence you to change your mind?'

'Just—dinner?' She searched his expression for any hint of mockery, and found none.

'I've reserved a table at Hobson House in Parnell,' Matt informed her with remarkable imperturbability. 'The food there is excellent. Now, be a good girl and go and change.'

'Oh, very well,' Karen agreed reluctantly.

He was impossible, she muttered beneath her breath as she inspected the contents of her wardrobe seconds later, sliding the hangers back and forth as she tried to make up her mind what to wear. It was still very cool at night—perhaps the three-piece suit in finely-woven wool? Its full skirt with matching waistcoat and tailored jacket was elegant and very fashionable, and teamed with a cream silk blouse it would dispense with the necessity to take a coat.

After a quick shower, Karen donned fresh underwear and slipped on the blouse, then the suit. A quick glance in the mirror confirmed her choice, and she hurriedly attended to her make-up and hair, then slipped her feet into knee-length boots.

'I'm ready,' she announced quietly as she entered the lounge a short while later, and met his slightly quizzical expression with a bland smile, watching as he rose to his feet with an almost animal grace.

In the car she sat in silence, aware of the broad darkly tanned hand on the gear-shift, the quiet strength of the man at her side. What would it take, she wondered idly, to ruffle that seemingly inflexible composure? She'd seen anger flare briefly in those dark tawny eyes, and instinct warned that when roused it would be swift and deadly.

The restaurant was well patronised, and it appeared that Matt was well known, for a table was found for them in a secluded corner.

'Will you allow me to order for you?'

Karen directed him a stunningly sweet smile and inclined her head. 'Why not?'

'Hmm,' he murmured sardonically. 'From a defiant firebrand to an amenable angel. One can only wonder what wrought the change.'

'Perhaps the fact that you might leave if I anger you?' she offered tentatively, a sparkle lighting her vivid eyes. 'I'd hate to be consigned to kitchen duties in lieu of settling the bill.'

Matt's eyes held a devilish gleam as he laughed softly. 'Do you have any particular dislikes?' he queried, indicating the menu.

'Not with regard to food, no.'

His soft chuckle brought a tinge of pink to her cheeks, and she deliberately refrained from looking at him.

After a starter of prawns in a delicate sauce, the waiter placed a plate containing a generous quantity of crumbed scallops, delicately-cut french fries, an elegantly-arranged platter of assorted salad greens, together with a choice of two sauces.

'What happened to upset you today?'

Karen paused, holding the fork poised halfway between her plate and her mouth. 'Apropos what?' she queried carefully.

'You recoiled from our accidental impact and took off with as much speed as a frightened doe bent on escape from an armed hunter,' Matt intoned wryly.

'You're—imagining things,' she refuted quickly, refusing to meet his gaze.

'No,' he accorded evenly. 'But you're obviously not going to tell me what caused it, so we'll change the subject. Lisa returned north with her grandmother yesterday, I believe?'

'Yes—Mother left for Whangarei mid-afternoon.'

'And she's due to return just before school resumes?'

Karen nodded. 'Yes, but I'll see her at the weekend. I intend driving up there on Friday afternoon.'

'Can you alter that arrangement?' Matt queried, eyeing her intently.

She met his gaze unflinchingly. 'Is there any reason why I should?'

'The long-range forecast is for relatively fine weather,' he informed her tolerantly. 'I had thought of taking my launch down to Pakatoa Island for the weekend. I'd like you to come with me.'

The implications involved in accepting such an invitation flashed through Karen's head in glorious Technicolor confusion the instant before she opened her mouth to refuse.

'With Lisa, of course,' Matt added, and she shot him an extremely doubtful look. 'Possibly your mother wouldn't object to bringing her down towards the end of the week,' he continued thoughtfully. 'If such an arrangement isn't convenient, then you can have Friday off to drive up and collect her.'

'I don't think so. Thank you,' she added, reluctantly meeting his gaze.

'Oh, Karen,' he mocked gently, 'surely you're not afraid to come with me? We'll be adequately chaperoned.'

'By a five-year-old child?' she queried with open scepticism.

'Yes.'

'No,' she refused firmly.

'If it will make you feel any safer,' he drawled, 'invite your mother to come as well.'

'You don't give in, do you?' she queried wryly. 'You'd

do much better to invite someone else. I don't imagine you lack for feminine company.'

'No,' he confirmed dryly, shooting her a penetrating glance, and she retaliated flippantly,

'It's simply a question of consulting your "little black book", isn't it?'

'I want *you*,' Matt declared deliberately.

'Well, you're not going to have me,' she said wildly.

'Will you ring, or would you prefer me to do it?' he countered, smiling at her speechless expression. 'Dessert?' he mocked quizzically. 'I can recommend the cheesecake. And coffee—black, or white?'

Karen didn't deign to reply—her voice seemed locked in her throat, and for what remained of the evening she confined herself to brief, monosyllabic replies to any conversation he offered.

They left shortly after ten, and as Matt chose to drive home along the waterfront, Karen let her gaze wander out over the dark ocean towards the north shore suburb of Devonport. It was a clear night, the sprinkling of stars high in the sky seemed so far away and therefore minuscule, and there was a strange magical pull that was strictly of the senses.

One part of her wanted nothing further to do with this inimically compelling man, and yet she longed for the joy of love—the strength of emotions that bound a man and a woman together for a lifetime. Then she gave herself a mental shake—such thoughts bordered on madness. There was no reason to suppose Matt Lucas looked upon her as anything other than a diverting challenge—someone to pursue and claim, briefly. She still bore the scars from one encounter with love— why place herself in a position to invite further heart- ache?

CHAPTER FOUR

'YOU'RE very quiet.'

Karen turned her head slowly, focussing her eyes on that broadly-etched profile a short distance from her own, then saw to her surprise that the car was stationary in her driveway.

'I was caught up with thoughts of my own.'

'Lunch tomorrow?' Matt suggested quietly, and when she shook her head, he demanded softly.

'Why not, Karen?'

'I—don't want to see you again.'

At the faintly desperate sound in her voice, he turned in the seat so that his face was only inches away, then he leaned forward and touched his lips briefly against her temple.

Karen felt herself begin to tremble, and when she edged away to move further back against her seat, he caught hold of her chin and tilted it so that she couldn't escape. Gently he traced her lower lip with his thumb, probing it open as his mouth travelled down over the delicate planes of her face to the edge of her mouth.

'Please—don't,' she whispered fiercely, and heard him give a soft laugh the instant before his mouth covered hers.

It was a tantalising kiss, tender yet with a hint of controlled passion, making no demands, but laying claim to something she didn't dare think about. Her will to resist slowly ebbed, and of their own volition her hands crept up to wind round his neck. His lips began an exploratory trail up over each cheekbone, then travelled down to tease an earlobe before tracing the pulsing cord at her neck. Her murmur of protest went unheeded as he slipped open the buttons on her blouse, and only when his hand slid beneath the silky material to expose a creamy breast did she struggle upright. Dear God, what was she thinking of? It had to be some form of temporary insanity to lie here like this, giving the impression she was willing to succumb.

'Let's go inside,' Matt suggested quietly, but panic welled to assume alarming proportions, making her both angry and afraid.

'No,' she gasped vehemently. *'No!'*

Matt regarded her searchingly, and his silence had more effect than words. A slight smile lifted the edge of his mouth, and he cupped her chin, raising her face until she was forced to look at him.

'That—embrace we shared moved you just as much as it did me,' he said steadily. 'Why pretend otherwise?'

'What does that prove?' Karen countered with a trace of bitterness. 'Other than that you're an expert in the art of seduction.'

'Who hurt you, Karen?' he queried gently. 'Your husband?'

'That has nothing to do with you,' she flung tersely, and felt the grip on her chin tighten as she tried to move out of his grasp.

'Why can't you accept that I want——'

'To help me?' she finished bitterly, then she laughed hollowly, her eyes glittering in the semi-darkness. 'Don't you mean yourself, by persuading me to go to bed with you?'

He was silent for several seconds, then he slowly shook his head. 'There's such a thing as waiting until you're asked,' he chided quietly, and she gasped in utter fury,

'You deny you're leading up to that?'

'I find the thought of making love to you infinitely provoking,' Matt enlightened wryly. 'But I happen to like my women willing and eager—not angry little kittens with their claws unsheathed.'

'I hate you!' she raged, almost choking with anger.

'It's about time you had some of the treatment you've been handing out,' he accorded, unperturbed, and she swung her hand towards his face, only to have it caught in a bone-crushing grip inches before it reached its target. 'And I dislike physical displays of temper.'

Karen felt the prick of angry tears behind her eyes, and she blinked rapidly, willing them to disappear. She wanted to cry and rage, both at the same time, like a frustrated wilful child.

'I'll see you to the door,' Matt said enigmatically, releasing her chin.

'It doesn't matter,' she managed shakily as she reached for the door-clasp, but he was already sliding out from the car, and he reached her side as she stood to her feet on the concrete driveway.

With the aid of the porch light she fumbled in her bag for her keys, conscious of a strange bereft feeling. She was so mixed up emotionally, it didn't bear thinking about. The key turned in the lock and she reached forward to switch on the light before swinging back to face him.

'Don't say anything, Karen,' he drawled. 'I'll see you tomorrow.' His expression assumed sardonic amusement as her eyes widened with disbelief. 'Lunch, remember?' he mocked. 'One o'clock, in the downstairs' foyer.' Leaning forward, he bent his head and bestowed a brief hard kiss on her unsuspecting mouth, then he straightened and strode briskly down the path to the car.

Much to Karen's relief, Susan chose to ignore her the following morning, and it made for a relatively harmonious working atmosphere. Mike failed to put in his customary appearance, and for that she was relieved, for she didn't fancy being on the receiving end of his verbal barbs.

As one o'clock drew near, she began to have qualms about lunching with Matt, and she deliberated whether to slip away a few minutes early to avoid him. Knowing his tenacity, he'd just as likely come to the house this evening if she didn't meet him—and that was the last thing she wanted. Given a choice, she'd prefer to see him briefly during the day.

There was a sudden quickening in tempo of typewriter keys, and she didn't need to look up to determine why. Who else but the Director himself? she thought wryly. He, who rarely graced the typing pool with his presence, was strolling calmly towards her desk, his expression a polite mask.

Why pick on me? she wanted to scream. But her voice was carefully controlled when he paused in front of her desk.

'It's not quite one yet. I'll be with you in a few minutes.' What was she saying, for heaven's sake? Whoever heard of a mere typist keeping the big chief waiting?

Matt surveyed her downbent head with wry amusement. 'The completion of that particular chore doesn't look devastatingly important to me. But who am I to dissuade such diligence?'

When he made no effort to move away, she spared him a cross glance which had no effect whatever, and it was to her credit that she made no typographical errors before releasing the paper from the machine. With un-flurried ease she checked the letter for errors, then placed it in the out-tray.

'I'm ready.' She stood up, collected her shoulder-bag, and placed the cover over the typewriter.

Matt's eyes gleamed with ill-concealed humour. 'You mean you don't intend to keep me waiting any longer? No make-up to freshen—or hair to fix?'

Karen shot him a level glance, then stepped round her desk and began walking towards the door, not really caring whether he followed or not.

'Was it something I said?' he mocked musingly, his hand reaching for the doorknob an instant ahead of her, and she deigned not to answer until they were clear of the foyer and almost to the car.

'Did you *have* to come into the office to wait for me?' she questioned in a tight little voice, and felt incredibly angry when he began to chuckle.

'Ah, so that's it!'

'I've already been the recipient of two verbal lashings on the undesirability of becoming involved with you,' she stated wryly, then laughed a trifle harshly. '*Involved?* If only they knew how fast I'm trying to run away from you!'

Matt waited until they were seated in the Jaguar, then he turned to regard her steadily. 'What makes you think I won't catch you?'

Karen could only look at him speechlessly. She opened her mouth, then shut it again, only to have her lips part in a soundless cry when his fingers trailed pro-vocatively over her heaving breasts.

'So much anger,' he mocked softly, 'when you can't be sure my intentions are honourable—or otherwise.'

'It could only be *otherwise*!' she erupted wildly. 'Oh, why can't you leave me alone?' she beseeched, almost on the verge of angry tears.

Matt regarded her in silence for several seconds, then he leaned forward and switched on the ignition. The car sprang to life, its engine an imperceptible purr, and it was only when he turned left at the first major intersection that she voiced tightly,

'If you'll be so good as to stop, I'll walk back and collect my car. I don't want to have lunch with you—the food would choke in my throat!'

'Kissing you into silence doesn't seem to have much effect,' he mused cynically. 'I'm sorely tempted to haul you across my knee and slap your delightfully-shaped derriere.'

'If you dare to lay a hand on me, I'll—I'll——'

'You'll—what?'

'Hit you back as hard as I can,' Karen vowed furiously.

'My dear Karen,' he drawled, sparing her a dark gleaming glance, 'be warned of the consequences of such an action. There's only one way it could possibly end—and entertain no doubts,' he added dryly.

Her eyes widened, dilating with remembered fear, and conscious of the painful thudding of her heart, she forced herself to breath evenly, slowly, in an effort to effect some measure of control.

'Please—take me back,' she pleaded at last, when the silence seemed to reverberate inside the car, accelerating the tension between them until she could stand it no longer.

'We're going to Antoine's for lunch,' Matt stated

grimly. 'I can hardly harm your virtue in a room full of people.'

Karen stared sightlessly out of the window, all the anger draining away as she became lost in thought. She didn't want to argue any more—in fact, she felt weary, a weariness that was mental rather than physical.

The restaurant was charming, and well patronised. Matt was greeted by name, and with a deference that was flattering. Karen thought his social life must be extremely active to command such attention, although she had to concede the man at her side accepted it with complete urbanity.

Throughout the meal he kept up a steady flow of sophisticated small-talk that required only a brief rejoinder, and to Karen's surprise it was almost two o'clock when she put down her empty coffee cup and spared a glance at her watch.

'Do you mind if I smoke?'

She looked up, faintly startled, then shook her head. 'Of course not.'

'More coffee?'

'No, thank you.'

She watched as he flicked the slim gold lighter and applied the flame to the cigarette held between his lips. The sight of that sensuously-moulded mouth brought a vivid reminder of his kiss—was it only last night? The memory made her shiver. There was a certain danger in continuing an association with a man of Matt Lucas' calibre. He possessed undoubted charm, an undeniable animal magnetism that most women would find difficult to resist.

'Will you have dinner with me tonight?' Matt queried with equanimity, and she answered quickly—too quickly,

'I don't think so.'

He regarded her thoughtfully for several seconds. 'Why not, Karen?'

She gazed at him helplessly. 'We've been over this before.'

'So we have.' He drew on his cigarette, then slowly exhaled the smoke. 'I can't quite fathom whether it's me—or what I represent.'

She didn't say a word, and it said a lot for her equilibrium that she managed to hold his gaze.

'Shall we say seven?'

'I had other plans for this evening,' she said desperately, and he smiled.

'Would it make any difference to your decision if I were to include my sister and her husband?'

Karen regarded him silently for several minutes, then began emotively, 'Why must you persist in asking me out? I've told you——'

'Countless times, I know,' he completed with sardonic amusement as he reached forward and stubbed out his cigarette. 'The trouble is,' he drawled, 'your words are at complete variance with what your kisses convey.'

A slow delicate colour tinged her cheeks. 'That's not true,' she whispered shakily, and saw his eyebrows raise in silent mockery.

'Shall we go?' he queried smoothly, standing to his feet in one fluid movement, and rather hesitantly she followed suit.

The fresh air outside cooled her cheeks and did much to assist a severely shaken composure, and in the car she chose to retain a silence he seemed to condone during the ten minutes it took to reach the apron of bitumen adjoining Consolidated Electronics.

'I'll call for you at seven.'

Karen paused, her hand on the door-clasp, and the look she cast him held a certain exasperation. 'Perhaps I should change my tactics,' she inclined with a sigh. 'If I became a clinging vine, I'm sure you'd drop me like the proverbial hot cake!'

Matt's laugh was low and faintly seductive. 'That image has interesting overtones, although I can't guarantee its success.' His voice continued persuasively, 'Mrs Rogers will be disappointed if you don't come. She'd planned on serving some tempting fare.'

'I——'

'Seven o'clock, Karen.'

'Very well,' she capitulated wryly. 'Don't call for me, I'll use my car. It's hardly necessary for you to make a double trip.'

Matt shook his head in a gesture that denoted mocking amusement, and she escaped before he had the opportunity to say anything further.

With complete feminine vanity, she elected to embark on a shopping spree—with the purchase of a new dress in mind. Not that her wardrobe wasn't adequately filled, but she felt she needed the added assurance a new garment would provide. Besides, the shopping excursion would occupy the empty hours remaining of the afternoon. Some time spent beneath the skilful hands of a hairdresser would bolster her morale, but first she'd select the dress.

After much deliberation she elected to shop in Parnell Village, and after visiting several boutiques she chose a skirt that fell in graceful folds from a gathered waistline and a waistcoat in matching *challis*. It was in soft tonings of beige, cream and brown, and with it she teamed a full-sleeved blouse of cream silk. Elegant slim-heeled sandals in matching beige completed the outfit, and as an added touch she bought an artificial rose to pin on her shoulder.

. Next came the hairdressing salon, and in a moment of impulse she decided on a sophisticated bouffant style, which when effected over an hour later caused the stylist to proffer effusive admiration.

It was almost six o'clock when Karen unlocked her front door, and after unpacking her purchases she made straight for the bathroom. With considerable care she took steps to protect her hair, then stepped beneath the shower to emerge minutes later feeling refreshed. Her toilette completed, she sprayed Lanvin's *Arpège* fragrance in the hollow between her breasts, beneath the lobe of each ear, and to the pulse at each wrist. Then she donned wispy underwear, a flounced slip, and began to apply her make-up with care.

At precisely fifteen minutes to seven she gently closed the front door behind her, and slipped into her car. She felt well equipped to deal with the evening ahead—and the shamelessly masterful man who was to be her host.

There were no other cars parked in the driveway when she arrived, and for a moment she considered returning home. Then sanity prevailed, and she made her way towards the main entrance.

Seconds after her ringing the bell, the door was opened by a smiling Mrs Rogers, and her greeting was genuinely warm.

'Do come in, Karen. Matt is——'

'Right here,' a deep voice drawled from directly behind her, and the housekeeper turned with a light laugh.

'I'll leave you, then.'

'Come through to the lounge,' Matt bade amiably, at

once the attentive host, and Karen allowed herself to be led across the wide hallway.

'Would you care for a drink?' he asked as soon as they entered the lounge, and feeling the need for some added courage she inclined her head in acquiescence.

'A light sherry will be fine.'

She watched as he crossed to the liquor cabinet, and her eyes followed the smooth actions his hands effected. He looked incredibly well groomed, his dark brown suit with its fine pin-stripe the epitome of male sophistication, the cream silk shirt and dark tie a superb complement. He possessed an undeniable attraction, a virility that was impossible to ignore.

As he crossed back to her side, she took the finely-cut crystal glass with its amber-coloured liquid from his hand and murmured a polite word of thanks.

'Janine and Jason will be here around seven-thirty,' Matt told her, adding somewhat mockingly, 'Also my mother.'

At once her lashes swept upwards, her eyes dilating with surprise.

'The entire Lucas family,' he revealed sardonically.

'I see,' Karen managed faintly, unsure what to make of this revelation. As the minutes ticked by she thought he wasn't going to add anything at all by way of conversation, and she found it increasingly difficult to hold his gaze.

'Have you contacted your mother about the weekend?'

The question shouldn't have surprised her, but it did. 'No,' she denied defensively. 'She'll expect me to arrive early Friday evening.'

Matt's eyes never left her face as he said evenly, 'If you'll let me have the number, I'll call her.'

'Now?' she queried, faintly incredulous.

'Why not?' he parried, one eyebrow raising in quizzical amusement at her expression. 'Shall I place the
call, or will you?'

'I wasn't aware that I agreed to go.'

He regarded her silently, his scrutiny intent. 'I've
reserved two adjoining units—one to accommodate
the three of you, the other for myself. All quite re-
spectable,' he mocked. 'And with your mother and Lisa
for company, you'll be quite safe from my—er—sus-
piciously-regarded intentions.'

An angry retort bubbled to the surface, and she refrained from voicing it with difficulty. 'You're incredibly obstinate,' she accused shakily. 'Anyone else would
have——'

'Given up?'

'Yes—*yes*!'

Matt viewed her fine fury with something akin to
amusement. 'I'm a determined man, Karen,' he stated
indolently. 'And I usually get what I want.' He leant
out a hand and gently tapped her chin. 'Let's place that
call to Whangarei—you can finish your drink afterwards.' His smile was warm and persuasive, and after a
few seconds she let out a sigh that defied description.

'Oh, all right. I'll ring.' Quite why she was giving in
when the last thing she wanted was to spend an entire
weekend with this disturbing man was beyond her
comprehension.

When she wished her mother to be out, Grace Ingalls
answered on the second ring.

'Mother—it's Karen,' she found herself explaining
unnecessarily, for who else would call from Auckland?

'Darling,' Grace rushed anxiously, 'there's nothing
wrong, is there?'

'No—no. How's Lisa?'

'She's fine. But that isn't why you've rung, surely?'

'I—no. It's just that I've received an invitation to go away for the weekend,' she elaborated hesitantly, acutely aware of Matt's presence less than two feet away. 'A—friend has this boat—a launch, actually, which he's taking down to Pakatoa Island this weekend. He'd like to include you and Lisa——'

'*He?*' Grace interrupted, her voice sharp with excitement. 'You mean a *man*, darling? Why, that's marvellous. Who is he?'

Karen flicked Matt a speaking glance, aware that he could hear every word her mother was saying. He, darn him, smiled with genuine amusement and moved closer until his arm was brushing against her shoulder. Childishly she pulled a face at him and turned her back, which was worse, for he retaliated by pulling her against him and holding her so that she couldn't escape.

'Didn't you hear me, Karen?' Grace queried plaintively.

Oh lord, she was being attacked from both sides! 'Yes,' she answered quickly. 'It's Mr Lucas.'

'Lucas? Would that be Matt Lucas—the man Lisa has been talking about?' Grace's voice rose a fraction. 'Your boss?'

The receiver was taken from Karen's hand before she could give an answer, and her efforts to snatch it back were evaded with an ease that was galling.

'Mrs Ingalls? Matt Lucas,' Matt said smoothly. 'Karen and I would like both you and Lisa to accompany us. We'll be staying on the Island—you'll be my guests, of course. I'd like to get away Friday afternoon, if possible. You will come?' He paused momentarily, listening to Grace's acceptance. 'Good. You'll get the

bus down on Friday morning? I'll pass you back to
Karen.'

Karen's hand was visibly shaking as she took the receiver from him, but it was anger at his high-handed-
ness, and when she finally replaced it moments later,
she was so furious she could hardly speak.

'Did you have to link our names together like that?'
she snapped resentfully as she struggled to escape from
his arms. 'Deliberately let her think—— Oh!' The ex-
clamation was a cry of anguish as she felt his lips touch
the side of her neck, and she twisted in vain, hope-
lessly trapped.

Firmly Matt turned her round to face him, and then
his mouth was on hers, warm and gently probing, part-
ing her lips, his touch disruptively sensual as he deepened the embrace with undoubted mastery.

She wanted to cry out, but no sound would come.
Never, not even once, had any man kissed her quite like
this. Nothing but the present held any importance. She
was a floating, mindless spirit, impassioned with the
ecstasy his touch evoked, and her response was in-
voluntary.

Interminable minutes later he gently trailed his lips
up to bestow a butterfly kiss to each closed eyelid, then
he rested his cheek down on top of her head. His arms
held her lightly, and when she tried to disentangle herself his muscles tightened fractionally.

'Don't move.'

The words were little more than a softly-murmured
directive, but she was powerless to resist, and she let her
body relax against his, becoming conscious that her
hands were still linked around his neck. Slowly she let
them slide down to rest on his chest.

Minutes later Matt gently put her at arm's length,

then tilted her chin, surveying her features with a thoroughness that brought warm colour to her cheeks. 'You look—bemused, and a little bewildered.' He bent down and kissed her gently. 'Trust me, Karen—just trust me, hmm?' A smile creased his features. 'You've not a vestige of lipstick left.'

What was happening to her, for heaven's sake? She felt totally devastated—weak-limbed and trembling, and her lips tingled with an exquisite pulsing warmth. Rather shakily she withdrew a compact and lipstick from her bag and attempted to repair her make-up. Her hand was far from steady, and she gave a start when Matt took the lipstick from her hand and tilted her chin.

With a few deft movements he stroked her lips, then solemnly regarded the result. 'I like you better without this artifice,' he murmured musingly, then glanced up at the sound of muted melodic chimes. 'That's the front doorbell, heralding the arrival of Janine, Jason, and Mother.' He caught hold of her elbow and directed a quizzical smile upon her downbent head. 'Shall we go out and greet them?'

The remainder of the evening passed in a daze, although Karen was aware of joining in the conversation and laughing at Janine's rather droll sense of humour. Exactly what she ate didn't register, apart from the fact that it was pleasing to the tastebuds. Both Janine and Mrs Lucas sought to put her at ease, and they succeeded, but in spite of their efforts she found it impossible to relax, for she was supremely conscious of Matt never far from her side. She had the feeling he was making a silent declaration to his family, and she couldn't help wondering why.

It was almost midnight when the others made a move

to go, and Karen stood to her feet with alacrity, determined not to be left alone with Matt. From the faint mockery evident in the glance he slanted towards her, he was aware of her reason, and his softly-murmured—'there's always tomorrow' echoed tauntingly all the way home.

Karen spent the following morning in a state of suspended trepidation, expecting a telephone summons from Matt to meet him for lunch, but one o'clock arrived with not so much as a glimpse of his powerful frame.

Emerging into the warm spring sunshine, she smoothed back a lock of flaxen hair and slid open the zip of her bag for the keys to her car. A quick glance at the parked cars was sufficient for her to note the absence of Matt's XJ-S Jaguar, and she slid in behind the wheel of her Datsun feeling vaguely disappointed.

By six o'clock that evening the telephone had rung precisely three times, but not one of the calls was from Matt. He was probably dining out with some gorgeous female, Karen decided wryly, and was loath to determine why such a thought should make her feel so restless and dispirited. She tried to assure herself that she'd have refused his invitation to dine even if he'd asked—but the knowledge that he hadn't rankled more than she cared to admit.

Clearly she had to occupy the lonely evening ahead, and for the first time in years the prospect of staying home was distasteful. On the spur of the moment she reached for the telephone and dialled several digits.

'Barbara? Hi—it's Karen,' she indicated brightly as soon as Barbara answered. 'Are you doing anything tonight? I thought I might come over for a while—that is, if it's convenient?'

'You're a lifesaver,' Barbara's voice chuckled down the line. 'Here I am playing the role of grass-widow again—yes, Bruce is down in Wellington—and I'm thoroughly sick of my own company, and these four walls surrounding me. I feel like going out!'

'How about taking in a movie? Can you get a sitter for Tania?'

'Yes—in answer to both those questions. Lisa's up north with your mother, isn't she? Why don't you pack a toothbrush and stay here overnight? It will save you going back to an empty house alone.'

It seemed ideal, and Karen didn't hesitate. 'You're on,' she accepted laughingly. 'I'll pick you up in half an hour.'

The fact that Matt might call, either by telephone, or in person, and expect to find her home didn't bother her a whit.

The film was a comedy that had them rippling with laughter from start to finish, and after coffee they drove home and gossiped over a glass of wine until almost one o'clock before opting to retire for the night.

'By the way, how is the illustrious Matt Lucas?'

Karen paused fractionally in the action of spreading jam on the slice of toast on the plate before her. 'Fine, as far as I know,' she answered carefully. 'Why?'

The glance Barbara directed across the breakfast table was decidedly roguish. 'I take it he's discovered that you work for him?'

'I've seen him within the confines of Consolidated Electronics—yes.'

'What about outside the office?' Barbara persisted. 'Have you been out with him?'

Barbara and Grace Ingalls should get together, Karen groaned, for their penchant for weeding out information and dissecting it was remarkably similar. Aloud, she asserted with deliberate cynicism, 'I've been wined and dined on more than one occasion—lunch as well as dinner. He's a very charming, sophisticated man—too sophisticated,' she added. 'And I have absolutely no intention of becoming involved with him.'

'Hmm,' the other mused speculatively. 'You're protesting just a shade too vehemently. Matt has a reputation for being dynamic with the ladies—if he's decided he wants *you*, Karen, you'll have one hell of a fight trying to resist him.'

Karen declined to comment. She bit into her toast, sipped her coffee, then adroitly changed the subject.

At eight-thirty she reversed her car out of Barbara's driveway, proffering a friendly wave as she sent it heading towards the main thoroughfare. As usual the traffic was heavy along Remuera Road, and there were times when the pace slowed to a crawl, demanding total concentration.

It was something of a relief to turn off into the side street that led to Consolidated Electronics, and she entered the parking area and eased the car into a vacant space.

The in-tray on her desk was filled almost to the point of overflowing, and Karen sifted through its contents and placed papers in order of priority. At least she wouldn't have time to think about the coming weekend, or wonder just when Matt would contact her to confirm their arrangements.

In that instant the intercom on her desk gave an insistent bleep, and Karen tried to ignore the way her pulse leapt as she depressed the button.

'Mrs Ingalls? Mr Lucas would like to see you.'

'Now?' Karen found herself asking, and Pamela Anderson rejoined smoothly,

'Yes. He has an appointment at ten.'

It was quite ridiculous to feel like a Christian about to be fed to the lions, but there was little she could do to dispel the feeling as she mounted the stairs, and her nervousness increased as she stepped into his office and closed the door behind her.

Matt's broad figure detached itself from a vantage point near the window, and he moved towards her with a litheness that was akin to animal grace. Dark tawny eyes surveyed her with an intentness that brought faint colour to her cheeks, and his expression became faintly quizzical as he leant against the edge of his desk.

'You wanted to see me?' Karen's voice sounded vaguely timid, and it angered her that he had the power to make her feel so—adolescent.

'I would hardly summon you to my office otherwise, Karen,' Matt intoned dryly.

If only he would say what he had to say, and get it over and done with! She felt at a distinct disadvantage and very much aware of his superior position—which he undoubtedly intended, darn him! He was playing with her as a cat might play with a frightened mouse, and it brought forth a latent anger she found difficult to control.

'I don't practise mental telepathy,' she managed evenly when she could bear the silence no longer, and she saw Matt's mouth twist into a cynical smile.

'More's the pity,' he drawled wryly, and extracting a slim case from his jacket pocket, he flipped it open and took out a cigarette, then lit it. 'Tomorrow's arrangements, Karen.' He exhaled the smoke with evident enjoyment and leaned against the edge of his desk to regard her thoughtfully. 'It's a two-hour trip, and I'd like to reach the Island before dark. Can you be ready at three?'

Karen considered the query, inwardly longing to declare she'd changed her mind and wouldn't go. However, Grace was involved, and no doubt Lisa was a bundle of anticipated excitement over the proposed weekend away—it would be unfair to give in to an entirely selfish motive and spoil their enjoyment. She murmured an affirmative assent, adding, 'Mother and I will provide whatever food is required.'

'That's not necessary,' Matt declared. 'There's a first-class restaurant on the Island.'

'Is there nothing we can bring?'

'Just yourselves,' he responded lazily. 'And don't forget to pack a swimsuit. The sea's too cold at this time of year, but there's a heated pool.'

Karen nodded, then turned towards the door. 'I'll see you tomorrow.'

'Why not have dinner with me tonight?'

'Thank you—no,' she refused evenly. 'I'll need to pack.'

'Until tomorrow then,' he mocked, and his eyes gleamed with hidden laughter as she escaped from the room.

CHAPTER FIVE

'DARLING, I'm dying to meet your young man,' Grace enthused within minutes of stepping through the front door shortly before noon the following day.

'Mother,' Karen protested. '*Young* hardly describes a man well into his thirties, and Matt Lucas is not *my* man, so don't read anything into the relationship. He's just my boss.'

'Bosses don't usually ask one of their typists *and* her family for a weekend cruise on their launch,' Grace observed dryly.

Karen could only look rather helplessly at her mother. She recognised the way Grace's brain was ticking over, and was at a loss to refute her logic. Matt would more than meet with any parental approval, and the fact that he already had Lisa in his pocket—figuratively speaking—would earn him full marks with Grace. She drew a deep breath and expelled it slowly. The weekend looked like being fraught with tension—and maintaining a carefree front was going to take all her energy. If Matt took more than a casual interest in her, she'd kill him! He had only to hold her hand in public, or smile disarmingly, and Grace would be dreaming of wedding bells! It was bad enough having to suffer normal speculation, without heaping fuel on to the fire!

'Let's have lunch,' she countered smoothly, glad of Lisa's presence. 'I've made some chicken soup, and I thought we could have an omelette to follow.' She smiled down at her daughter. 'Will you help Gran set

the table? The soup is ready, and I've only the omelette to make.'

Lisa commandeered the conversation during lunch,
and while the dishes were washed and dried. Her excitement seemed to mount with each passing minute, and
most of her questions had to remain unanswered as
neither Karen nor Grace could supply much information about Pakatoa Island, the size of Matt's launch,
where they would cast off from, and countless other
details which Lisa considered needed clarification.

At a few minutes past three the Jaguar drew to a
whispered halt in the driveway, and Lisa blithely ignored Karen's injunction to stay inside the house. She
flew out the door and ran down the steps towards the
car, to be caught in Matt's arms and swung high into
the air amidst giggles of delight and deep masculine
laughter. The action brought a sparkle of conjecture to
Grace's eyes, and caused Karen's lips to purse with
frustrated anger.

'Where's the boat?' Karen heard Lisa query breath-
lessly as she deposited two suitcases out on to the
porch.

'All ready and waiting for us at the Half Moon
Bay marina,' Matt responded patiently as he lowered
the little girl down to the ground.

'Is it in the water?'

'It is.' He indicated the man who was emerging from
the passenger seat. 'This is Ben Rogers. He's coming
with us to look after the launch while we're on the
Island.'

Karen reached his side with Grace a short step behind,
and she effected the introduction with a politeness
that caused Matt to raise a mocking eyebrow.

'Karen seems intent of being formal,' he smiled,

offering his hand to Grace. 'Please call me Matt.'

'And you must call me Grace,' the older woman returned with a warm smile, and to say she was taken with the inimicable Matt Lucas was an understatement, Karen decided wryly, for her mother positively sparkled, exuding sufficient feminine charm for both of them.

Ben Rogers stowed their luggage in the trunk, then slipped behind the wheel just as soon as Karen and Grace had seated themselves either side of Lisa in the rear of the luxuriously-appointed vehicle.

The drive to Half Moon Bay was achieved in less than fifteen minutes, and Karen was thankful that apart from a few brief monosyllabic words she offered in direct reply to Matt's queries, she was able to leave the bulk of the conversation to her daughter.

There were several boats of various sizes moored at the marina, and it came as no surprise when they made their way along the jetty towards a large cabin-cruiser whose sleek lines and trim exterior denoted both wealth and pride of ownership. The interior was as opulently furnished as compact utility would permit, and Karen managed a tight smile as her mother and Lisa made appropriate complimentary comments.

'If you'll excuse me, I'll assist Ben in getting under way,' Matt indicated, and as soon as he had moved out of sight Grace bestowed on her daughter a beautific smile that Karen had learned to dread.

'Darling, he's gorgeous! And all this——' she spread her hands eloquently to encompass the cabin. 'Lisa is obviously smitten—and that's more than half the battle.'

The battle had only just begun, if she did but know it, Karen thought perversely. Aloud, she chided,

'Mother, I warn you—don't begin a matchmaking campaign. If you so much as dare to voice one of your subtly-unsubtle hints, I'll do something regrettable!' Her eyes flashed blue ice, and Grace raised a fluttering hand in self-defence.

'I was only offering my considered opinion,' she said in a hurt voice, and Karen sighed.

'I can assure you that there's nothing behind Matt's invitation, so let's just enjoy the weekend ahead.'

It was perhaps as well that Matt chose to return at that moment with Lisa in tow, and with determined effort Karen set herself the task of being an amusing, talkative guest. The glass of sherry Matt handed out minutes later helped considerably, and she endeavoured to ignore the teasing, faintly-mocking laughter barely hidden beneath his gleaming gaze.

The throbbing engines reached full pitch, then settled down to a steady beat as they urged the craft out into the upper harbour towards the Hauraki Gulf.

Beneath Matt's informative commentary, they observed the passing mainland through the cabin portholes, took interest in the small island on their left named Motuihe, and immediately following, the large populous Waiheke Island measuring twenty miles in length and abounding in picturesque coves and bays, sandy beaches and rocky promontories. To the east of Waiheke lay a parcel of islands that had been briefly sold in a package deal to a group of intending settlers who sailed across the Tasman on the brig *Rosanna*.

'The original Deed of Purchase, held by the Mitchell Library in Sydney,' Matt divulged with a smile, 'was never taken up, as a canoe-load of Maori warriors brandishing shrunken heads frightened the prospective immigrants away, and Ponui Island, the largest of the group, has been owned and farmed by the Chamberlin family since 1853. Pakatoa, the furthest distant in the group, was purchased by a large cinema-owned franchise, and developed in the mid-1960s as a sophisticated tourist resort.'

The light was beginning to fade as they reached Pakatoa, and their first glimpse of the Island revealed an expanse of sandy beach to the right of a long jetty that protruded far out from a sheltered cove. A belt of pine trees both to the east and west of the main resort provided an effective wind-break, and as the launch slowed to minimum speed and slipped in to the east side of the main jetty, it was possible to view the manicured lawns surrounding the main block of buildings.

'We'll disembark here, then Ben will take the launch round and drop anchor out from the main beach,' Matt announced as he led the way up on deck.

'Where are we staying, Matt?' Lisa queried engagingly as he swung her on to the jetty.

'One of those units to your left,' he indicated with a smile as he stood by to give first Grace and then Karen a steadying hand.

'Oh, look, there's a trampoline!' Lisa cried with excitement as they reached the end of the jetty and stepped on to the bitumen road leading towards the main building.

'I'll go through to the office and register,' Matt declared. 'Perhaps you'd both like to show Lisa the swimming pool, and I'll join you in a few minutes.'

Lisa skipped along between Grace and Karen, her small face wreathed with smiles as they emerged into the courtyard containing a large tiled pool. There were gaily-coloured beach umbrellas, several brightly-covered

chaise-longues, and numerous tables and chairs. Shrubs
in large painted wooden tubs were spaced to provide
contrasting colour, and there were banana palms and
decorative pebble gardens. Totally enclosed by Lock-
wood-constructed buildings which housed a shop on
one side, a recreation hall at one end, a lounge and
bar, and flanked by a take-away bar and restaurant, the
effect was distinctly tropical and designed to encourage
guests to enjoy a lazy carefree holiday.

'This is really something, don't you agree?' Grace
commented, and Karen nodded in silent acquiescence.

'Can we swim tomorrow?' Lisa begged, her large eyes
round and expressively pleading.

'If it's warm enough,' Karen qualified cautiously.

'There's not a breeze to be felt,' Grace commented,
glancing round with interest. 'This area is totally pro-
tected from the elements. I must say Matt is very
generous insisting we stay here as his guests.'

Karen refrained from endorsing her mother's sentiments. There was a reason behind his benevolence, and
she didn't intend to shock Grace with the revelation—
at least, not yet. No doubt she'd be provoked into
doing so in the near future—especially if Grace continued to extol Matt's supposed virtues!

'Here's Matt now,' Lisa cried, and Karen felt bound
to protest——

'You really shouldn't call him by his first name, Lisa.'

The little girl's face sobered into an expression of
puzzling uncertainty. 'But, Mummy, he said I could
call him Matt. Truly he did.'

'I'm sure it's all right, dear,' Grace intervened
smoothly, and Karen felt defeated.

It was bad enough having to fight a mental battle
with him, without having her mother and Lisa join

forces against her as well. She watched as he strode towards them, his broad well-muscled frame and rugged countenance exuding a forceful vitality that was impossible to ignore.

'We're on the western side,' Matt declared as he joined them. 'I'll lead the way.'

A short walk from the courtyard they reached a long ranch-styled building divided into self-contained units.

'Units five and six,' he informed them as he mounted the short flight of steps on to a wooden verandah. 'They're identical, but perhaps you'd like to choose?'

The query was directed to Karen, and she managed a slight shrug. 'It doesn't matter. Which would you prefer, Mother?'

'Can we have number five?' Lisa broke in happily. 'That's how old I am.'

'That settles it,' Matt laughed. 'Five it is.' He put the suitcases down, inserted a key into the lock, then stood aside for them to enter.

Karen met his slightly mocking smile as she passed him, and was tempted to poke out her tongue. His eyes gleamed with devilish laughter, and she wrinkled her nose in a gesture of retaliation.

'It's got a kitchen,' Lisa piped in surprise, and Matt leant out a hand to ruffle her hair.

'So it has. But we won't be eating here.' He swung his gaze to encompass both Karen and Grace. 'Our table is reserved for six-thirty. There's no need to get changed, unless you particularly want to, for the management stress informality. I'll collect you at six, and we'll have a drink in the lounge before dinner.'

'Thank you, Matt,' Grace inclined warmly, and as soon as he disappeared into the adjoining unit she crossed towards the bedroom. 'I adore this natural wood panelling, don't you? It gives the rooms a feeling of warmth. Which bed would you like, darling?' she queried of Karen. 'I don't mind where I sleep, if you'd like Lisa in with you.'

'Can I sleep out here?' Lisa begged, looking longingly at the television, and Karen shook her head.

'Oh, no, young lady,' she grinned. 'I'm wise to that lark. You can share the bedroom with Gran, and I'll sleep out here on the divan.'

'Are you going to change, Karen?'

She looked down at her tailored trousers rather doubtfully. They were fashionably smart, and hadn't creased at all. However, a dress would probably be more suitable. 'Yes.' She spared a quick glance at her watch. 'Lisa, go into the bathroom and wash, there's a good girl. I'll unpack, as it will save time later.'

'I don't think I'll bother with mine,' Grace declared. 'I'll probably come back fairly early with Lisa. I'll do it then.'

Karen shot her a discerning look, for she knew that nonchalant tone. 'You wouldn't be concocting a scheme whereby Matt and I can be together later this evening? Don't,' she advised evenly. 'When Lisa is tired, I'll bring her back and put her to bed.'

'Oh, darling, grow up,' Grace chided. 'Matt will expect to spend some time alone with you. Why else would he invite me along, if not to supervise Lisa?'

Karen stifled the quick retort that rose to her lips, and crossed the room to pick up both suitcases. 'I'll put yours in your room, shall I?' she suggested, and not waiting for an answer, she took them into the bedroom and began to unpack.

'Mummy, do you want me to change?'

Karen looked up from the task at hand and gave a

smile. 'Well,' she considered thoughtfully, 'It will get quite a bit cooler later on in the evening. Perhaps you could wear your long skirt and a jumper. I'll carry your cardigan just in case you need it.'

'What are you going to wear?'

'My batik shirt—the long one, and a jumper,' she answered promptly. It was casual, yet afforded a sophistication she felt she needed whenever in Matt's presence.

'If you're both going to change, then I think I shall, too,' Grace declared. 'How much time do we have?'

'Twenty minutes,' Karen revealed.

When Matt knocked on their door they were ready, and he viewed their appearance with a quizzical smile. He'd changed his shirt and added a jacket, and the total effect was one of disturbing masculinity.

The lounge was well furnished, with numerous armchairs and tables at evenly-spaced intervals. A few young children were grouped in front of the television as they viewed a popular programme, and towards the rear of the room a few chairs were occupied with guests enjoying a leisurely pre-dinner drink.

Lisa accepted a glass of lemonade, and when the glass was empty she wandered towards the television leaving the adults to their conversation.

Matt appeared totally relaxed—every inch the urbane host, Karen conceded wryly from her vantage point a few feet distant. He set out to be charming, and succeeded without any effort at all. Grace succumbed with an alacrity Karen found difficult to condone, and she longed for the evening to end.

It wasn't so much what he did, or even what he said, that she took exception to—but her mother seemed to notice every little gesture, every smile, and by the time they entered the restaurant for dinner Karen was con-vinced Matt had deliberately contrived to give Grace the impression that their relationship was other than platonic.

Because of Lisa's presence, Karen was forced to hold her tongue, and by the time they'd consumed their meal and were lingering over coffee, her face felt quite stiff from maintaining a constant smile.

They emerged from the restaurant and at Lisa's sug-gestion began wandering towards the recreation room. A quick glance inside revealed a group of teenagers attempting a complicated dance routine to the sound of pop music emitting from a jukebox in one corner, while at the far end of the room two junior-sized bil-liard tables both had games in progress.

'Shall we go into the lounge for a drink?'

Grace was quick to assent. 'What a good suggestion, Matt.' She cast her daughter a stunning smile. 'All right with you, darling?'

There wasn't much Karen could say, although she longed to refuse. 'Just for a while,' she allowed politely, and deliberately refrained from meeting Matt's prob-ing gaze. If she hadn't know better, she might almost have suspected a conspiracy between Matt and Grace—instead, she was up against their individual determin-ation, which combined, was fast proving to be formid-able!

After a short while Lisa began to show visible signs of tiredness, and with total lack of guile she shifted from her chair to sit beside Matt. Within minutes her head drooped against his arm, and Karen stood to her feet with the intention of retrieving her.

'Sit down, Karen,' Matt advised as he gently transferred the little girl into his arms. 'She can sit on my lap for a while.'

'I'll take her back to the unit and put her to bed,' she protested, but he shook his head.

'Soon—if you must. Meanwhile, she's quite comfortable where she is.'

Grace manufactured a discreet yawn which didn't fool Karen in the least. 'I'm feeling rather tired myself,' she said. 'I'll take Lisa. You two stay and enjoy yourselves.'

Mother! Karen cried silently, shooting Grace a quelling glance that had no effect whatever. Showing remarkable calm, she stood to her feet. 'Thank you, but I'll take her.' She turned towards Matt and addressed the top button of his shirt. 'If you'll excuse me?'

He, darn him, stood to his feet with Lisa cradled against his chest. 'Let's make it unanimous.' The look he slanted her held mocking amusement, and never had she felt more like screaming with angry frustration.

At the door of the unit Matt bade them goodnight and relinquished Lisa, and Karen let out a sigh of relief when the door closed behind him. She carried Lisa through to the bedroom, undressed her with care and slid her pyjamaed figure between the sheets, then tucked the blankets around her recumbent form. Tidily she folded the little girl's clothes, a slightly puzzling frown creasing her forehead.

'Did you bring Lisa's cardigan back, Mother?' she queried quietly. 'I gave it to you to hold after dinner.'

Grace looked momentarily perplexed. 'I must have left it in the lounge. I remember putting it down beside me, but I didn't have it in my hand when we came in just a few minutes ago.'

'I'll go back and see if I can locate it,' Karen offered. 'It should still be there.'

It was dark outside, and away from the illuminated perimeter surrounding the long block of units Karen quickened her step. She could hear the muted sound of music and laughter mingling with the steady buzz of conversation as she neared the lounge.

A customary clutch of nervousness lifted her chin a fraction and she forced a slight smile to her lips. Self-confidence had always been a mantle she'd had to assume with conscious effort whenever it became necessary for her to confront a group of people alone. Call it a too-generous amount of sensitivity, she mused distractedly as she hovered in the doorway of the large dimly-lit room.

The chairs they'd occupied were still empty, but she couldn't see any sign of the missing cardigan. It had most likely been handed in at the bar, and with a sigh of resignation she made her way down the length of the room, becoming aware as she walked of the several pairs of male eyes following her path, and she steeled herself to walk in a calm unhurried manner.

Several men lined the bar, and she stood to one side, reluctant to gain their attention.

'Can I buy you a drink?'

Karen turned at the query, and met the openly-suggestive stare with dismay. Eyes eloquent in their appraisal left her in little doubt that he wanted much more than just the sharing of a drink.

'The name's David. What's yours, sweetheart?'

She turned away, not bothering to answer him.

'Don't be hasty, beautiful,' he taunted softly, and she swung back to stare at him with cool detachment.

'Thanks for the offer of a drink, but I came here to retrieve a cardigan.'

'I'm sure you could manage something—*kahlua* is fairly innocuous,' he persisted, exercising practised charm. Reaching out, he took hold of her elbow and summoned the barman.

'No,' she refused firmly, extricating her arm, and his eyes narrowed.

'Hey, I'm a generous man, honey. Stay with me, and I'll give you a good time.'

'I've already refused. Must I be rude?'

'Come on, what's the harm in sharing a friendly drink?' he taunted. 'Why come in here alone if——'

'The lady isn't alone,' a familiar voice drawled quietly from behind, and Karen felt a tide of relief wash over her as her accoster gave an eloquent shrug and faded away.

The look she flicked Matt was one of gratitude. 'I could have coped—but I won't say your arrival wasn't timely.'

He considered her thoughtfully for what seemed an age, then he smiled and indicated the bar. 'Would you like a drink?'

'I should get back. Mother——'

'Grace knows I came after you.' Leaning forward, he lifted a hand to touch her cheek. 'Don't look so—anxious,' he chided softly. 'You're quite safe.'

Was she? Her emotions were constantly at war where he was concerned. Out of desperation, she ventured, 'How did you know I was here?'

One eyebrow rose quizzically. 'I remembered Lisa's cardigan—first you had it in your hands, then Grace, throughout the evening. Yet when I bade you good-night, neither of you were carrying it. Logically, it had been left behind, so I decided to check.' His smile did strange things to her equilibrium. 'Sure enough it was on the chair, and I returned it, only to learn from Grace that you'd discovered the loss and had gone to retrieve it yourself.'

'Thank you,' she murmured belatedly.

'For what, Karen?' he mocked gently. 'Rescuing you?'

A delicate pink tinged her cheeks, much to her chagrin. 'For retrieving Lisa's cardigan.'

'Let's have that drink,' Matt suggested dryly.

Summoning every ounce of calm, she queried coolly, 'Do you play billiards? The table is free, and——'

'Anything would be better than sitting in a secluded corner with me?' he intercepted quizzically.

To treat him lightly was the only way she could retain her sanity. 'Well, I do fancy pitting my questionable skills against yours in a game of billiards,' she slanted. 'And alcohol will only impair my ability to cue the ball.'

Tawny eyes gleamed down, sparkling with amusement. 'What if I win?'

'No forfeits,' she refused, shaking her head at him. 'For all I know, you're probably an expert.'

'No moonlight stroll along the beach afterwards? Shame on you, Karen.' His teeth showed white between his lips as he uttered a soft laugh, and she sobered quickly.

'If you wanted a warm and willing bedmate,' she said evenly, 'you invited the wrong girl.'

His voice when he spoke was both dry and inflexible. 'Let's play billiards, before I'm tempted to shake you.'

Matt won, as Karen expected him to, but not by too great a margin—although she suspected he deliberately missed several shots to lighten his score.

'A quick drink, I think,' he mused. 'Before the bar closes.'

She sat next to him as she sipped vermouth and lemonade, her eyes ostensibly on the images flickering across the television screen. Never had she been so aware of him. His mere nearness set her heart racing erratically and affected her breathing. With one arm draped over the top of her chair, he had only to move fractionally towards her and they would touch. If she could just close her eyes and lean back—pretend the past didn't exist, that Brad Ellman had been a figment of her imagination. She wanted to meet Matt's eyes and smile, to respond freely without fear or inhibition.

A soundless gasp escaped her lips as Matt took hold of her chin and she wasn't quick enough to mask her feelings before he turned her face and caught a glimpse of her unguarded expression. His lips curved slowly into a warm smile and assumed a gentleness that brought a lump to her throat.

'I must get back—it's getting late,' she stumbled over the words in her agitation, and he released her chin and stood to his feet.

Karen felt strangely apprehensive as they left the lounge and began walking along the path that led to their respective units.

The look he slanted down at her was unreadable in the darkness, and she gave a strangled gasp as he caught hold of her hand and spread her fingers between his own. 'What do you intend doing about another job?'

'I thought I might go back with Mother for a few days,' she managed calmly, fighting the urge to snatch her hand away. 'Lisa has another week of holidays before returning to school.'

'You'll be back in Auckland by the weekend?'

'Why?' she queried baldly.

'I have tickets for a charity dinner next Saturday. I'd like you to come.'

'I may not be back in time.'

'Karen, you perverse little baggage,' Matt laughed softly, turning her towards him. 'Why do you constantly fight against me?'

She was silent for so long as words stuck in her throat. At last she queried, 'Why me, Matt? Why not someone else?'

'I've asked myself the same question several times during these past two weeks,' he revealed wryly. 'Will you come?'

'Where?' she murmured distractedly, and gasped as his hands caught hold of her shoulders. There was no way of avoiding that sensuous mouth as it descended to cover her own in a kiss that set her on fire and turned her limbs into a shaky, jelly-like substance that seemed incapable of holding her upright.

'Now, will you come?' he teased gently, and laughed softly as she buried her head against his chest.

'You don't play fair,' she choked in response.

'That's tantamount to an admission of sorts,' he chuckled, then sobered to continue seriously, 'Lisa can stay with Mrs Rogers. Rest assured she'll be well looked after.'

'That's not necessary,' Karen found herself protesting.

Matt's eyes gleamed with sudden devilry. 'My home is large, with several spare bedrooms. Why not stay over? You could take Lisa home the following day.'

She stiffened involuntarily and strained against him. 'I'll arrange for a babysitter.'

He was silent for a long time before putting her at arm's length. 'Don't tar all men with the same brush, Karen.'

She felt her stomach give a sudden painful lurch. 'What do you mean?'

He smiled a trifle wryly. 'I don't need extra-sensory perception to determine that you've been badly hurt in the past. At a guess, I'd hazard it has to be Lisa's father.'

'You know nothing about it,' Karen choked huskily.

'No,' he agreed, lifting her chin to meet his steady gaze as he admonished softly, 'Don't presume to judge me, or my actions, by another man's—cruelty.'

She wasn't capable of uttering so much as a word, and when they reached the steps leading to each respective unit he leant down and kissed her—a brief, hard kiss, that bore little resemblance to gentleness.

'Goodnight, Karen.'

Saturday dawned fine and mild, with a slight breeze blowing in from the sea. The sky was almost clear, with only a few small puffs of cumulus cloud to contrast white with blue.

They ate breakfast in the restaurant at eight, then at Matt's suggestion they embarked on a walk round the island's foreshore.

Lisa was in her element, being with the two people she adored most in the world. She and Matt seemed to share a natural empathy, and it was fast becoming obvious that she regarded him with affection—which fact Grace was quick to point out to her daughter.

Karen had slept badly, having been plagued with dreams that had reached nightmarish proportion, so vivid that she'd emerged into wakefulness only to slip back into a continuation of subconscious torment. There was a strange, haunted quality that deepened her eyes and lent a pensive air to her expressive features. She wished with all her heart that the weekend was over, and the light of day had lent determination to her resolve not to see Matt again. It was his probing, disturbing manner that was responsible for her present anguish, and the sooner she could return to her former calm existence, the better. Already she had broached to her mother about returning north to Whangarei for much of next week, and had expressed the desire to leave after lunch on Monday. Explaining why she'd chosen to resign from her job had taken some ingenuity, but for once Grace had held her tongue and accepted the explanation given.

After a light lunch they returned to their units to change into swimwear, although Grace elected to observe rather than participate. Karen caught a mirrored glimpse of her slender curves in a one-piece costume of slinky black arnel, and was well pleased with the effect. Her bikini had been left at home in her unwillingness to parade a scantily-clad body beneath Matt's piercing scrutiny.

The pool itself was virtually unoccupied, although there were several guests stretched out on deck-chairs enjoying the warm spring sunshine.

'Mummy, hurry up, please,' Lisa begged. 'The water looks deep, so I'll have to wait until you get in.' She sat at the pool's edge with her feet dangling in the water, and her eyes brightened with pleasure as Matt lowered his length down beside her.

'Come on, infant,' he bade warmly, slipping into the water and holding out his arms. 'In you come.'

Lisa needed no second bidding, and seconds later her giggles turned into infectious laughter. 'Your chest is tickling me.' She dissolved into delicious chuckles, and Matt began to shake with silent mirth as he lowered her gently into the water.

'Can you swim?'

'Of course I can,' the little tot responded with pride. 'Watch me!'

Karen descended the steps into the heated water and met the faint mockery evident in his eyes. She was all too conscious of him attired in hip-hugging briefs that exposed long muscular thighs, a broad chest liberally covered with water-darkened hair, and well-muscled shoulders. Sporting a suntan that had obviously been acquired during his European trip, he exuded virile masculinity from every nerve and fibre.

With determined effort Karen concentrated on giving Lisa her undivided attention, although it was difficult to ignore Matt when Lisa constantly vied for his approval. Together they swam, one either side of the little girl, the length of the pool, then Matt emerged and lifted Lisa to stand beside him before leaning down to offer Karen his hand.

It was too cool to dry off beneath the sun, and they towelled themselves briskly before walking to the changing-rooms to don their clothes.

Matt was deep in conversation with Grace when Karen returned with Lisa skipping happily along at her side, and she joined them rather self-consciously—which was ridiculous, she chided rather angrily. She should be immune from the deep curling sensation his steadfast gaze evoked whenever those tawny eyes rested upon her. His touch, his voice, had the power to turn her into a spineless wreck, and that knowledge irked her unbearably. Instinct warned he wasn't another Brad, but to trust Matt spelled sure disaster—something her scarred emotions couldn't hope to cope with. No doubt he regarded her as something of a challenge because she hadn't succumbed to his charm with the alacrity to which he was accustomed. A liaison with any man was the last thing she wanted, and to allow Lisa to become too fond of him would only be cruel.

A family disco for the evening's entertainment was prominently advertised on the management notice board, and despite frantic sign-language from Karen to the contrary, Grace offered her services as babysitter.

'I'm sure Lisa would enjoy watching for an hour or two,' Matt remarked with seeming indolence. With studied ease he extracted cigarettes and lighter from his shirt pocket, then took time to light up, expelling a slim column of smoke with evident satisfaction. 'I don't think children should be entirely isolated from participating in their parents' social activities.'

But you're not a parent, Karen longed to protest—and you have no right to manipulate my life through Lisa. She shot him a wrathful look that had no effect whatsoever, for he merely smiled. Oh, he had a skin thicker than a rhinoceros!

'Do you play cards?' Grace queried in an attempt to direct the conversation into safer channels. 'Perhaps we could arrange a game for later in the evening, if Karen refuses to relegate Lisa into my care.'

It was a decided barb, and Karen felt hurt that her mother should resort to sarcasm—and none too subtle, at that!

'There's no need for either of you to organise Lisa over my head,' she managed quietly. 'It should be left for me to decide when she goes to bed.' All of a sudden she felt the need to escape—anywhere would do, as long as it was away from Matt and her mother. With that in mind, she stood to her feet. 'I'll take Lisa down to the trampoline for a while.' She didn't wait for either of them to comment, but stepped quickly towards the recreation room where Lisa had wandered to only minutes before.

The little girl came happily enough, and together they skirted the pool area and made their way past the main entrance and crossed the lawn.

Fortunately only one of the trampolines was in use, and Karen lifted Lisa up and stood back to watch as her daughter began to bounce up and down.

'This is fun!' Lisa called delightedly, and Karen smiled as the tot tried to emulate some of the actions executed by a boy on the adjacent trampoline.

Darn Matt Lucas, Karen cursed shakily. She should never have come. Stupid tears welled up in her eyes, and she blinked rapidly to control them. Grace was in her element playing the role of matchmaker, and it mattered little whether her daughter was a willing participant or not.

'Matt!' Lisa cried excitedly. 'Matt—look at me!'

Oh no! Karen groaned beneath her breath. She wanted to turn and rail her fists against his broad chest—in fury against him, her mother's single-mindedness, fate, and the world in general. If there was some way she could get off the island before tomorrow ... But such an action would be childish, and unwarranted.

'Grace is only trying to make it easy for you to enjoy yourself,' Matt drawled quietly from behind, and Karen stiffened defensively.

'She's indulging in a matchmaking campaign,' she

argued bitterly. 'And you, aware of it or not, are abetting her.'

'Surely she can't be blamed for wanting your happiness?' he queried, and she retorted swiftly,

'I *am* happy!'

'Are you?'

His mocking amusement was the last straw. 'I was, until you began trying to take over my life,' she flung with intended sarcasm.

'Steady,' he warned. 'Whatever will Lisa think if she sees her mother giving way to a temper tantrum?'

'Go to hell!' she retaliated violently.

'I suggest we postpone this—discussion, until a more appropriate time,' Matt drawled silkily.

'There's nothing to discuss.'

'No? Let's agree to differ on that point for the moment.'

Karen turned to look at him, holding his gaze with determined effort as she fought for some measure of control. For once she wished they were alone so that she could fling all the angry words she had bottled up inside.

'I'm on my way out to the launch to check over a few things with Ben,' Matt informed her quietly. 'I'll be back in time for dinner.'

She nodded, not trusting herself to speak, and he turned and walked towards the beach. She watched as he slid a dinghy down the sandy foreshore to the water's edge, then he stepped agilely into it and began handling the oars with ease, sending the tiny craft towards the luxury launch anchored several hundred yards out from shore.

'Mummy, can we have another swim?'

Karen brought her attention back to her daughter.

Lisa had scrambled down from the trampoline and was standing less than a few feet away. 'Yes,' she agreed, giving a warm smile as she caught hold of the small hand. 'Our swimsuits will be wet, but who cares?'

They enjoyed a pleasurable afternoon—Karen all the more so due to Matt's absence, and Grace, with an unusual display of astuteness, didn't so much as mention his name.

Dinner was a leisurely meal, during which Matt maintained a companionable flow of conversation, and afterwards they strolled down to the jetty, enjoying the cool evening air for a while before wandering back to the lounge.

The chairs had all been rearranged round the walls to allow space for dancing, and stereophonic equipment was in the process of being set up ready for the disc-jockey to operate. Already there were several guests standing in groups waiting for the evening's entertainment to commence.

'Matt—darling!'

Karen turned slowly, curious to see who was heralding the man at her side with such provocative seductiveness. A vision of fascinating femininity in the shape of a tall willowy brunette was gliding—there was no other word to describe her fluid movement across the floor—towards them. The soft crêpe-de-chine blouson top worn over limb-hugging knee-breeches, together with long sueded boots, were attention-getting and quite outrageous, but the girl displayed undoubted flair and the panache of a professional model. Her make-up was flawless, her hair sleekly pulled back into a deceptively simple knot.

Exotic perfume tantalised the nostrils as she paused close to Matt's side, and with a total lack of inhibition she reached up and kissed him in a manner that caused Karen to squirm with embarrassment.

'Berenice,' Matt accorded with a degree of laconic mockery. 'Friends of mine,' he accorded by way of introduction. 'Grace Ingalls, her daughter Karen, and granddaughter Lisa—Berenice Meyer.'

A smile flashed with sparkling warmth across the girl's features as her eyes swept from Grace to linger assessingly on Karen, before returning with a faintly teasing expression to Matt.

'When did you get back from Europe, you naughty man? I've been waiting for you to call me.'

'Two weeks ago,' he remarked sardonically, and smiled when she gave a pouting moue. 'I've been busy.'

'Playing Happy Families, darling? How—interesting, for you. We must get together some time for—dinner,' she indicated provocatively. 'I'm in the end unit overlooking the beach—drop in later for a drink.' Her eyes flicked towards Karen and Grace. 'Nice meeting you. 'Bye, darling.' She blew Matt a kiss, and with a faintly affected movement of her hand she slipped away towards the bar.

'What a—fascinating girl,' Grace breathed faintly, and Matt's mouth widened into a cynical smile.

'Yes, isn't she?' he agreed.

Karen glanced up at him, her expression solemn. 'If you'd like to join Berenice, Matt, please feel free— Mother and I won't mind. In any case, Lisa will be tired and ready for bed soon.'

His features were enigmatic, but there was a dangerous gleam in the look he directed her. 'Grace mentioned a game of cards, I believe—if you've no objection, of course?'

'Isn't that carrying chivalry a little too far?' she

parried sweetly, deliberately letting her eyes travel
to where Berenice was seated swinging back to meet his
gaze.

'I prefer your company,' he drawled softly, and she
had to stifle a faintly derisive laugh.

'I can't think why.'

'I have to admit to being rather confused by it myself,' he murmured lazily. 'Dance with me, Karen.'

'Are you asking, or commanding?'

'A little of both.' He caught hold of her hand and
drew her effortlessly into his arms. 'Hmm, you smell
adorable,' he complimented quietly. 'Let me guess—
Arpège?'

'You're quite an expert, aren't you?' Karen retorted,
cross with herself for being so susceptible. The lighting
was subdued, the music soft and dreamy—a subtle setting to which it was all too easy to succumb.

Five minutes later she gave a sigh of relief and
stepped back as the tempo changed and the lights
blazed to their brightest extent. 'I'll go and talk to
Mother for a while,' she indicated, unable to resist
adding, 'Perhaps Berenice would like to dance?'

'I doubt she'll lack for a partner,' Matt averred
smoothly, taking her hand in his, and he tightened his
grip as she tried to pull away.

By nine-thirty Lisa was visibly drooping, and she
went happily into Matt's arms when he suggested they
return to the unit. Karen's faint protests were ignored
as he carried the sleepy child, and he entered the unit
she shared with Grace to deposit Lisa down on to the
bed she silently indicated.

When Karen emerged some five minutes later after
undressing and putting the little girl to bed, Matt
was sitting opposite Grace at the dining-room table,

a pack of cards held in one hand.

'Grace suggests poker,' he indicated calmly. 'I refuse to gamble for money with my guests, so shall we settle for matchsticks as stakes?'

Later, Karen could only conclude that the whole thing had been carefully contrived with most of the blame being attributed to her mother, for in less than an hour Grace managed a series of yawns and retired after losing her hand—a little too obviously to be genuine.

'Karen will make you some coffee, Matt,' she declared, standing to her feet. 'It will only keep me awake. Goodnight.' She smiled first at Matt, then her daughter, and crossed to the bedroom she shared with Lisa, shutting the door firmly behind her.

The stakes Matt held were considerably more than those Karen had, and it seemed highly probable he'd win the game.

He did, with effortless ease, leaving her with three matches, and she looked at him enquiringly.

'Coffee?'

'Oh, come, Karen,' he smiled with a trace of mocking indulgence. 'Don't you want to try and win back at least some of your original stake?'

'What's the point?' she countered evenly, indicating her sadly-depleted pile.

'I could lend you sufficient to play another game.'

'I'd probably lose, and end up in your debt—then what?'

His eyes held hidden laughter. 'I guess I could come up with an idea regarding suitable repayment.'

'No, thanks,' she refused firmly.

'Pity,' he drawled, then gave a negligent shrug. 'In that case—coffee, black, with no sugar.'

Karen filled the electric jug with water, and while it heated she took down one cup and saucer, and spooned in instant coffee. As soon as it was ready she took it across and set it on the table in front of him. 'I haven't let the water boil—you'll be able to drink it without waiting for it to cool.'

'So anxious for me to be gone?'

'It's not late,' she responded. 'I don't imagine Berenice will be in bed.'

'And even if she is, it won't much matter, as doubtless I'll soon join her,' he drawled silkily. 'Isn't that what you mean to imply?'

Karen saw his eyes darken and felt suddenly afraid. 'She invited you to call in for a drink,' she defended in explanation.

'As I recall, I didn't accept.'

She shrugged, then gasped audibly as he reached out and caught hold of her hand. Exerting painful pressure, he pulled her round the table to stand immediately in front of him, then he drew her inexorably forward until she lost her balance and had to clutch at his shoulder to steady herself. He was still seated, but even so, his head was not much lower than her own. Forced to lean towards him put her at a disadvantage, and her strangled protest didn't gain any leniency.

With a single movement he stood to his feet and hefted her over one shoulder, fireman-fashion, then he walked to the door, opened it, and stepped outside. He seemed impervious to the blows her fists railed down his back, and by the time he had taken the few steps necessary to bring him outside his own unit, extracted the key and unlocked the door, she was quietly sobbing.

'You—unspeakable fiend! she bit out the moment he lowered her down to stand in front of him. 'I hate you!' She lashed out at him, hitting wildly.

'Stop it, Karen,' Matt directed brusquely, and catching hold of her shoulders he gave her an ungentle shake. 'I brought you here so we could talk with some degree of privacy. Anyone would think from your reaction that I intended to rape you.'

Karen felt the colour drain from her face as she looked up at him. Horror and fear were mirrored in her eyes for one brief infinitesimal second before she managed to gain control. She gazed at him sightlessly, unaware of those tawny depths narrowing sharply as they took in her whitened features and the vulnerable trembling of her mouth. Tears welled in her eyes, then overflowed to trickle slowly down her cheeks.

'Dear God,' he swore softly, then he took her chin between gentle fingers and lifted it so that she had to look at him. 'Karen——'

'Don't—please don't ask any questions,' she pleaded shakily, running the tip of her tongue along her lower lip.

'Karen, for the love of heaven——'

'Please—if you don't mind, I'd like to go now.'

He released her, letting his hands slide slowly down her arms. 'Will you be all right?' Gently he cupped her face and moved a thumb over each cheek, removing traces of dampness.

She nodded speechlessly, and he stood aside to let her pass, his expression one of brooding reluctance.

In the adjoining unit Karen locked the door behind her, then crossed to sink wearily down on to the divan. Sleep had never been more difficult to court, and it was a long time before she rose to her feet and began undressing for bed. The hours seemed long as oft-remembered images rose to haunt her, and once she came awake with a start to find the light on and her mother bending anxiously over her.

'You've been dreaming, darling,' Grace soothed, and Karen gave a despairing groan.

'I didn't wake Lisa?'

'No, she's sound asleep. Do you want a drink? Tea—coffee?'

'Tea,' she responded gratefully, sitting upright and reaching for her robe.

'I thought you were over these bad dreams of yours,' Grace observed minutes later as they sat at the table.

Karen grimaced slightly. 'They come and go, Mother.'

'Did you have a difference of opinion with Matt?'

'You could say that,' she shrugged wryly.

'Did he tell you he plans to get away after breakfast tomorrow? He intends calling in to Kawau Island for lunch.'

Karen tried to look interested—which was rather difficult at two o'clock in the morning. 'That will be nice,' she said faintly, and Grace cast her a speculative look.

'I think he's serious about you,' she offered. 'Why else would he invite you here for the weekend?'

'It wouldn't occur to you that it might be for the usual reason a man asks a woman to go away with him?' Karen mocked.

'If he hadn't included Lisa and me—yes,' Grace declared, and Karen had to laugh.

'Well, much as I hate to disillusion you—he fully intended it to be a cosy twosome. Only I wouldn't play ball.'

Grace looked slightly nonplussed. 'Oh,' she faltered.

'Shall we try and get some sleep?' Karen suggested. 'We'll need to be up early to pack before breakfast.'

CHAPTER SIX

KAREN'S initial greeting to Matt next morning when they met over breakfast was a polite dissembling that brought forth a gleam of amusement and caused him to shake his head in silent resignation.

Throughout the day she remained subdued, preferring silence, or at best, monosyllabic contribution whenever politeness demanded she converse, and only Lisa was able to raise a smile.

If Matt noticed the dark circles beneath eyes that were more deeply blue than usual, he made no comment, and after an enjoyable lunch at Mansion House on Kawau Island, he directed Ben to skirt around the island and head back to the mainland.

They disembarked at the Half Moon Bay marina, and as soon as Ben had deposited their suitcases into the boot of the Jaguar Matt drove them home.

Never had the distance to Remuera seemed so short, and the instant the car whispered to a halt in the driveway Karen slipped out and waited for Matt to retrieve their belongings from the boot.

'Won't you come in for a drink?' Grace encouraged in an effort to discount what she considered to be her daughter's lack of good manners.

'Thank you, Grace, but I'll take a raincheck, if you don't mind,' Matt declined. 'Ben will need my assistance for an hour or two.'

'It's been a very pleasant weekend,' Grace extolled with enthusiasm. 'You've been very kind. Thank you.'

Karen murmured an appropriate few words in a like

vein, then beckoned to her daughter, 'Come along, Lisa. Matt has to get back to the launch.'

'When will we see you again?' Lisa queried guilelessly, and Matt smiled with genuine warmth.

'Next Saturday. Your mother is having dinner with me.' He shot Karen a look that dared her to deny their date the following weekend.

'I'm going to miss you,' the little girl declared with earnest sincerity, and flinging up her arms she asked tentatively, 'Can I kiss you goodbye?'

In answer Matt swung her high against his chest for an affectionate embrace, then he lowered her gently to the ground. 'Have a nice holiday, poppet,' he bade softly, then with a brief salute that was meant to encompass both Karen and Grace, he slid in behind the wheel and reversed the car down the drive.

They were scarcely indoors when Grace voiced her disapproval, and it was more than Karen could stand.

'Please, Mother,' she begged. 'I'm tired, and I have an awful headache. No recriminations—I couldn't bear to hear them. Let's unpack, have a light meal, then indulge ourselves by having an early night.'

It didn't help that the heavens unleashed their fury soon after dusk, lashing the roof with rain and gusty winds that sent tree branches waving like giant arms in the night. An omen, Karen decided bleakly, as she turned up the switch on her electric blanket and gathered the covers more tightly around her.

Morning brought little respite, and the drive north took longer than usual, slowing speed to a cautious level that added more than thirty minutes on to the customary two-hour drive.

Coming home always brought a lump to Karen's throat, for there were so many memories—happy childhood ones she liked to remember, when her father was alive, and some she tried hard to forget. It seemed so recent, not anything like six and a half years ago since she'd left to go and live in Auckland, and driving through the familiar streets was like the turning back of a page in her life.

Over there, to her left, was the park where she first met Brad, the wooden bench she'd occupied during her lunchbreak when he'd approached her to ask the time. He'd ended up sharing her packet of sandwiches, and when she returned to work she had accepted a date for that same evening.

It was all here, a vivid painful reminder of the gullible fool she had been in believing his skilfully-acted lies. The restaurants where they'd spent many a dreamy evening sharing a candlelit dinner as they'd planned their future, the shops where she'd selected her trousseau.

There were familiar faces, friends, who even after such a passage of time, seemed over-solicitous whenever they saw her, and inevitably managed to have an eligible male in tow for dinner or at a party she felt honour bound to attend.

Karen sighed as she brought the Datsun to a halt in the driveway adjoining the neat suburban house that had been her home for so many years. She shouldn't have come, yet to have stayed in Auckland without the protective buffer Lisa's presence afforded would have been madness. For as much as she hated to admit it, Matt Lucas had crept beneath her skin, rekindling fires she'd thought could never spark alive again. The knowledge made her want to run and hide, like some frightened wild animal that was steadily being hounded into an inescapable trap.

'Let's get inside and light the fire,' said Grace. 'It's so cold and wet—and to think we were basking beneath the sun only the day before yesterday!'

Karen silently echoed her mother's sentiments as she bundled Lisa from the car, although half an hour later as she sat before the warming flames curling from the grate, and with a hot cup of coffee in her hand, she was inclined to view the situation much more pleasantly.

'Finish your coffee, darling. I must make some calls to let a few friends know that you're here.'

'Mother, don't accept any invitations on my behalf,' Karen warned quickly. 'I really need a quiet few days, not a social whirl.'

'Of course, darling,' Grace soothed. 'But I have to ring the boarding kennels about collecting Simone, and there are one or two people I must contact.'

No, Karen groaned, it's all starting again. Fifteen, perhaps twenty minutes from now, Grace would re-enter the lounge, her face wreathed in smiles, and there would be a dinner engagement they just couldn't get out of, a party being given on some pretext or other that they would be rude to refuse. Before nightfall, each day, each evening of her stay would be accounted for. Nothing could dissuade Grace—arguments, tearful rages, even flat refusals to participate had had little or no effect in the past, and after the first year Karen had quietly given up.

If only the next five days could somehow pass by some painless magical process. Pass they would, inevitably, but she would need every ounce of patience she possessed, and then some! If only she could maintain a sense of humour about the whole thing, it might not be too bad, she decided wryly.

So began a hectic week of social activity. Lisa commanded their attention throughout the day, and together they took in two cinema matinees, visited several places of interest, and spent an entire afternoon shopping for clothes.

It was the evenings Karen began to dread, although on reflection there was only one incident that rankled, with repercussions that were not wholly pleasant. The 'eligible man' presented at a midweek party was the perfect gentleman for much of the early evening, until several drinks loosened his tongue and aroused his passion. She managed to escape unscathed, but it added little to the already low opinion she held of the opposite sex.

The weather continued to be contrarily unseasonal, and Saturday dawned with the promise of yet more rain. Karen left Whangarei shortly after nine, with few misgivings about the drive ahead of her.

Sheets of rain continually lashed against the car, making for minimal visibility, and consequently driving became a hazardous exercise. The roads were well sealed and in good condition, but there was a passage that wound round the hills providing innumerable bends and winding curves that taxed driving skill and required total concentration.

By the time Karen reached the outskirts of Auckland she felt drained, and about as enthusiastic as a rag doll at the prospect of going out that evening. She had a headache, and longed for a hot bath and an early night. The thought of dressing up for a charity dinner in one of the city's most exclusive restaurants didn't thrill her at all—nor did indulging in the customary thrust-and-parry badinage she had come to expect with each encounter with the indomitable Matt Lucas.

Twice during the afternoon she hovered close to the telephone with the intention of ringing him to say she wouldn't go, and then at the last moment she changed her mind. The thought of his sardonic cynicism upon hearing she'd decided to opt out of the invitation only served to put her on her mettle.

At five-thirty Karen bundled Lisa into the car and drove the short distance to Barbara's, where she'd arranged for the little girl to stay overnight.

By the time she returned, she had little over an hour in which to shower and shampoo her hair, then dress. Matt was calling for her at seven, and if she was to be ready in time she'd have to hurry.

Ten minutes later she switched on the blow-wave and set about drying and styling her hair. It really needed a trim, for she rarely let it grow much below shoulder-length. Thick, it possessed plenty of body, and freshly styled it swung about her shoulders with the slightest movement of her head, almost as if it had a life of its own. Make-up came next, and apart from highlighting her eyes with two tones of eyeshadow, skilful application of mascara, she touched the blusher to her cheeks to give them some colour, and covered her lipstick with gloss. The total effect was pleasing. Now she had to make a decision between two evening gowns—one demurely simple in heavy cream silk, the other more daringly cut in a vivid sea-blue crêpe-de-chine.

After much deliberation she chose the blue gown, and had just applied a few dabs of perfume to each wrist and in the hollows at the base of her throat when a series of knocks on the front door heralded Matt's arrival.

'Good evening,' Karen greeted coolly, and glimpsed

his cynically raised eyebrow as she stood aside for him to enter.

'Am I late?' His eyes gleamed with sardonic humour, and she could quite cheerfully have ignored him—except that he wasn't a man any woman could successfully ignore or overlook. Impeccably groomed in a superbly-tailored dark suit, immaculate shirt linen, and a black bow tie, he looked dynamically masculine and the epitome of male sophistication.

'Shall we go?' she countered, determined to remain calm. He had the knack of ruffling her composure, and in his presence she was invariably goaded into behaving like a childishly immature adolescent. He confused her with a sensual finesse she'd not previously experienced, arousing desires deep within that she'd rather leave dormant. Somehow, she had the feeling she was the pawn in a game of chess—with Matt the master player.

'Dare I ask if you enjoyed your visit to Whangarei?'

Karen looked at the dark profile in the dim interior of the car, and was unreasonably irked by his cynical amusement.

'The weather was wet for much of the time, as you're no doubt aware,' she began stiffly. 'There were some outings we'd planned for Lisa's benefit that had to be postponed.'

'And you, Karen—did you indulge in any social activities?' he pursued, causing her to burst into retaliatory speech.

'Yes—I went out every night,' she snapped. 'And each time with a different man. I was wined and dined, and danced until dawn. I received no fewer than two propositions—and was harangued with bitter invective for being a frigid little bitch when I wouldn't comply,' she finished bitterly.

His soft chuckle was the very limit, and she rounded on him in utter fury. 'You can take me home. I don't even want to go out tonight, and especially not with you!'

'We're almost there,' Matt said quietly. 'The food promises to be excellent, the band good.' He eased the large car into the car-park and slid into an empty space, then switched off the engine and turned to look at her. 'Running away never did solve anything,' he added enigmatically, and she swung suspiciously bright eyes towards him.

'Just what, or whom, am I supposed to be running from?'

'Me,' he declared evenly, when a few painfully slow seconds had passed. 'You'd have been wiser to have stayed in Auckland and faced the inevitable.'

'By inevitable, I suppose you mean wearing down my resistance sufficiently so that you can bed me,' she accused scathingly. 'Chance is a fine thing—and you'll never gain it. Accept me as the one who got away.'

'My dear Karen,' he drawled silkily, 'you're like a little wild kitten—all claws, and bristling soft fur. You hiss at every hand extended—regardless.' His eyes held hers, unwavering in their scrutiny. 'Now, shall we go?'

An hour and two drinks later, Karen had mellowed sufficiently to feel oddly penitent for her outburst, and when Matt suggested she might like to dance, she complied without so much as a word.

'Such docility,' he murmured close to her ear as he drew her into his arms. 'You're like a chameleon. I'm almost inclined to ask if the real Karen Ingalls will please identify herself.'

'Don't bait me,' she begged, lulled into a pleasing yet dangerous inertia, whereby all she wanted to do was to drift slowly to the music. It was always the same, she thought ruefully. He possessed some strange magnetic chemistry that struck an answering spark deep within her, and fighting against it was fast becoming a losing battle.

When they returned to their table, the other four seats were occupied, and Karen wondered why she wasn't surprised to see Berenice Meyer among the occupants.

'Matt, sorry we're late, darling. You know how it is,' Berenice greeted Matt effusively, her lively dark eyes aglow. As an afterthought she turned to Karen. 'Hello—er—I'm afraid I've forgotten your name,' she declared with no hint of apology, before swinging her attention to Matt. 'You know Michael, don't you? And this is Andrew, and Mark.'

Trust Berenice to arrive with no less than three young men in tow, Karen accorded uncharitably. And she was gorgeously gowned, looking every inch the successful model she undoubtedly was.

Matt introduced Karen with accustomed ease, and when they were all seated he beckoned the wine steward.

Karen had begun to feel the effects of the alcohol she'd consumed by the time she finished the contents of her glass, for as yet no food had been served. Aware of Berenice's preoccupation with Matt, she permitted herself to be drawn into conversation with Andrew— or it might have been Mark. Exactly what they talked about she wasn't sure, for she was rapidly becoming resentful of the way Berenice was monopolising Matt. As much as she tried to convince herself she didn't care a jot, she couldn't ignore the slow burning jealousy that rose to the fore.

Dinner was in the form of a smörgasbord, and Karen viewed its announcement with relief. It was exotically presented in the large adjoining dining-room and guests were invited to take plates and cutlery, make their own selection, and return to their tables. Each dish proved to be a gourmet's delight, and she had to concede that the food was well recommended.

'Dance with me, Matt,' Berenice enticed within five minutes of completing the contents of her plate. 'I shan't have dessert—it's fatal in my line of business.' She smoothed hands down over her slight hips and gave a pouting moue.

Karen turned towards Matt and smiled sweetly. 'Go ahead.'

He ignored her directive, and queried calmly, 'Would you care for dessert?'

'No, thank you,' she declined with the utmost politeness. 'Do dance with Berenice. I'm sure she'll be quite devastated if you don't.' She gave a warm smile that didn't fool him in the least, for his eyes held a dangerous glint that boded ill if she didn't desist.

'Matt, come on,' the other girl enthused with deliberate seductiveness as she moved to stand close beside his chair. 'Karen doesn't mind.'

'Maybe later, Berenice,' Matt refused, unperturbed by her pout, and his smile was totally without warmth. 'I'm sure any one of your escorts will oblige.'

'I think I'll get some coffee,' Karen indicated in slightly strangled tones, and rose to her feet with the intention of putting some distance between herself and the potentially explosive situation that had arisen.

'Allow me.'

She looked up into those tawny eyes and could have stamped her foot in sheer anger. 'The only solution is for each of us to fetch our own.' Without a further word she walked away, uncaring whether he followed or not.

'Would you believe me if I said I had no idea Berenice was going to be here tonight?'

'Really?' Her voice was chillingly remote. She reached the table where coffee was being dispensed, asked charmingly for hers to be served black, then sugared it liberally before turning to face him. 'Would you like me to manufacture some excuse and catch a taxi home? I assure you I shan't mind.'

'You'll do nothing of the sort,' Matt declared evenly. 'When we've finished our coffee, we'll dance.'

'You're very good at giving orders,' she returned, resentful of his proprietorial manner. 'However, I don't work for you any longer.'

He gave her a level look that was infinitely more dangerous than any words he could have voiced, and in the end she had to glance away.

'I really do have a headache, and I would like to go home,' she said a trifle wearily. 'I had a long drive this morning in far from ideal conditions. I almost rang you twice during the afternoon to say I wouldn't come tonight.' She paused and raised a hand to smooth back a stray lock of hair. 'However, there's no need for you to curtail your enjoyment,' she concluded politely. 'If you'll be good enough to call me a taxi——'

'No taxi, Karen,' Matt intervened. 'I'll take you home, if that's what you'd prefer.' Taking a firm grasp of her elbow he led her towards the flight of stairs leading down to the main entrance.

Karen didn't offer a word as they walked to the car,

and she sat in total silence during the ten minutes it took to reach her home.

The instant the car drew to a halt in the driveway she reached for the door-clasp. 'Don't get out,' she declared hastily. 'I can let myself into my own house.'

He didn't answer, and slipping from behind the wheel he moved to her side and walked with her to the front door.

She needed a second attempt to fit the key into the lock, her hands were so shaky, and when the door swung open she turned and bade him a polite goodnight.

'Aren't you going to invite me in?' Matt queried mockingly. 'We haven't had much opportunity tonight to talk.'

'What is there to talk about?'

'I won't ravish you, if that's what you're afraid of,' he promised cynically, and she retorted angrily,

'I'm not afraid of you, and as for ravishing me—I wouldn't let you!'

He moved inside and shut the door behind him, then turned to regard her thoughtfully. 'Your—holiday hasn't improved your disposition.'

'It was no holiday,' Karen revealed obliquely. 'Grace inveigled several eligible young men to escort me to the cinema, to dinner—on any pretext she could invent, and with such skilful manipulation that nothing short of a temper tantrum would have excused me. I felt like a piece of horseflesh being paraded before bidders at an auction block!'

Matt's eyes gleamed with hidden laughter. 'Your vivid imagination is mind-boggling.' He leant out a hand and idly trailed his fingers down her cheek. 'Was it really so bad?'

'Yes! I had to suffer salacious looks, listen to improper suggestions, and elude enough wandering hands to put an octopus to shame.'

'Ah, Karen,' he murmured softly, and his hands caught hold of her shoulders, pulling her close. His head lowered down to hers, and his lips brushed gently against her forehead.

For a moment Karen almost relented, wanting nothing more than to lift her mouth to his, but a strange anger burned inside her, making her want to lash out and hurt in any way she could.

'Don't,' she refused hardily, twisting her head away and pushing against his chest with her hands.

'You're quite safe,' Matt declared evenly. 'A few kisses is all I have in mind.'

'Forgive me if I don't believe you. My experience of men hasn't taught me to believe in noble instincts.'

'Not all of us are predatory sexual animals,' he drawled. 'Sooner or later you're going to have to revise your opinion.'

Her head tilted back as she looked up at him. 'And you think I should begin with you? Where would that get me, Matt?' she queried bitterly. 'My heart's already been bruised and battered once. I've vowed no man will ever do that to me again.'

He looked down at her in silence, and there was little she could gauge from his expression. Each passing second seemed to increase the tension inside her, until she wanted to scream.

'Go to bed, Karen. I'll ring you tomorrow,' he said at last, and his conciliatory tone brought her anger to the fore.

'Stop treating me like a child!' she cried resentfully, 'Oh! I wish you'd go away and leave me alone. Lisa

and I were doing fine until you barged into our lives—
gaining her affection, and trying to——' she came to a
furious, stumbling halt. 'I don't want to see you again—
ever!' Angry tears sprang to her eyes and lay quivering against her lashes, and she turned away, unable
to bear his steady gaze a second longer.

It seemed an age before she sensed him turn and
begin walking away, and her shoulders slumped with
relief when she heard the front door click shut. Seconds
later the almost silent purr of the car's engine magni-
fied his departure.

Oh God, she sighed wearily, what have I done? During the past few weeks Matt had become part of her
life, and although she'd sworn never to let another
man get close to her again, he'd succeeded in tumbling
almost every barricade she'd erected in defence. Ironically, now that she'd told him to leave, she wanted
him to stay. She was such a puzzling mixture of emotions, she couldn't even rationalise any more.

She moved towards the kitchen in a daze, and
switched on the light, then reached into the cupboard
where she kept sundry medication. She longed for the
sweet oblivion sleeping tablets would bring, but having
had alcohol she daren't take any. Paracetamol would
ease her headache, and perhaps sheer weariness would
take care of the rest.

'Mummy, when is Matt coming to see us?'

Karen glanced across the table at her daughter, and
managed to keep her voice even. 'He's probably busy,
honey. He may not come today.'

Lisa looked momentarily disconcerted. 'But he said
he would, and it's already lunchtime. Will he come this
afternoon?'

Quietly she endeavoured to make light of the situation. 'Perhaps he thinks we're busy. After all, we have been away on holiday,' she explained. 'And tomorrow you start school.'

'Didn't he say if he'd come today?' Lisa queried doubtfully, and Karen answered carefully,

'No, Lisa, he didn't mention it.'

'He does like us, doesn't he, Mummy? We will see him again, won't we?'

Karen almost groaned out loud. This was becoming more difficult by the minute! 'I'm sure we will, honey, but he's a very busy man. He's been kind to us, taking us out, but we're just two among many of his friends. It's only fair that he should spend some time with them, isn't it?'

'I guess so,' Lisa allowed slowly, then asked with startling discernment, 'Don't you like Matt any more, Mummy?'

Karen felt robbed of speech, then she managed to counter tentatively, 'Would you mind very much if he didn't come and see us again?'

The little girl's lower lip began to tremble, and her eyes filled with tears. 'I like him—I like him a lot. All the other children in my class have daddies— I'm the only one who hasn't got one.'

Karen's heart turned over, and she bent down to gather the little tot into her arms. 'But darling, I've told you lots of times that you did have a daddy. He was killed in a car accident before you were born.'

Lisa's words were muffled against Karen's breast. 'Can't I ever have another daddy now?'

'Well,' Karen considered carefully, 'If I were to get married again, then whoever I married would become your stepfather.'

'Then I might have a daddy one day?'

'I guess you might,' Karen agreed hollowly, then she gave a laugh that was totally lacking in humour. 'Hey, I thought we were happy together, just you and me.'

'Do you think we could maybe visit Matt this afternoon?'

Talk about singlemindedness! 'No darling, I don't think we should do that,' she said slowly. 'But if you'd like to go out, we could visit the Zoo this afternoon. And on the way home we'll stop and get some take-out—fried chicken and chips. We could eat them in front of the television. Does that sound like a good idea?'

Successfully diverted, Lisa helped clear the table and tidy the dishes, then she changed into warm outdoor clothes and scrambled into the car to view the afternoon's excursion with excited anticipation.

Fortunately it wasn't raining, although there was a strong breeze that teased at the length of their hair and whipped warm colour into their cheeks. The zoological park proved to be a popular choice, for there were several families equally bent on strolling leisurely along the paths that led past numerous cages housing animals of various descriptions.

It was almost five when they returned home, and after a picnic-style meal in front of the television Karen suggested Lisa should have her bath, then they could play Monopoly until it was time for her to go to bed.

The following day Lisa resumed school, and the house seemed strangely quiet and empty without her presence. Restless for something to fill in the time until the little girl returned, Karen embarked on a spring-cleaning stint. With the prospect of seven weeks' end-of-year school holidays due to begin mid-December, she was reluctant to look for part-time employment until school resumed early in February. However, if she didn't find something constructive to do, the days would drag unbearably.

By Wednesday Karen had cleaned all the windows, both inside and out, until they positively sparkled behind freshly-laundered curtains. The kitchen cupboards were immaculate, and every inch of paintwork inside the house had been wiped down.

Thursday afternoon saw every drawer tidied, and a bag filled with clothes put aside to be donated to charity.

She was loath to admit that the reason for such relentless energy was Matt. She hadn't heard from him since Saturday, and she tried to tell herself that she didn't want to. So why was she feeling let down and more than a little disappointed? Perhaps he'd decided to take her at her word, after all. Somehow, the thought of never seeing him again plunged her into the depths of despair. She'd flung words at him that were unjustified—angry accusations that had little to do with Matt himself.

As soon as Karen had dropped Lisa off at school on Friday morning, she drove in to Newmarket and spent an hour selecting paint and vinyl wallpaper with which to redecorate the bathroom. It was the only room in the house that needed a facelift, and truth to tell, it could well have waited another year or two before requiring attention.

It was almost midday by the time she had sanded down the surfaces to be painted, and after a quick cup of coffee she draped protective covers over the bath, basin, and floor. A small step-ladder proved more cumbersome than she'd first supposed in the confines of the room, and she abandoned it for a chair draped with an old towel.

Attired in old jeans, an even older jumper, and a scarf tied over her hair, Karen worked with dedicated concentration until it was time to go and collect Lisa from school.

'Mummy, you do look funny,' the little girl giggled as she slipped into the front seat of the car. 'You've got spots of white paint everywhere—even on your nose!'

She hadn't paused to check her appearance before leaving the house, for there was no reason for her to get out of the car, so it didn't really matter.

At home, she paused long enough to give Lisa some milk and biscuits, then she disappeared into the bathroom with the hope of finishing the undercoating before she had to stop and prepare dinner.

'I'm going to watch television, Mummy,' Lisa informed from the doorway. '*The Flintstones* are on now.'

'Okay, honey,' Karen murmured abstractly, her attention taken with a piece of scotia-moulding. There, she'd almost finished—just one more section to do and the ceiling and all the mouldings would be completed. She stepped down and moved the chair further towards the corner, then stepped up again.

Somewhere between standing on the chair and reaching for the paint and brush she made an error in balance. The instant she felt the chair slip she flung out a hand to steady herself, uncaring of what she grasped. Unfortunately, the glass shelf bracketed on to the wall above the bath offered little support, and the next second she was falling towards the floor with an appalling lack of grace. Her outflung arm hit the side of the bath as she landed awkwardly on her side. For a brief second she felt no pain, only shock, and she half sat, half lay on the floor for several minutes before attempting to get up.

'Mummy, I heard a thump. Are you—oh——'

Karen tried to summon up a reassuring smile. 'Thump? I must have sounded like a herd of elephants! Still, it could have been worse—I could have been holding the tin of paint at the time. Then we would have had a mess. Oh, darn,' she grimaced slightly as the telephone began to peal insistently. 'Be a good girl and answer that for me. Tell whoever it is that I'll ring them back. Okay?'

Lisa looked incredibly anxious as she hovered uncertainly in the doorway, then she turned and ran down the hallway. Her voice was a frightened squeak and somewhat muffled, and Karen didn't take much notice as she concentrated all her efforts on rising from the floor.

Her leg didn't feel too bad—sore, but bearable. However, her left arm was one agonising ache, and she almost cried out loud as she endeavoured to move it. She couldn't have broken it, surely? Rather shakily she limped out towards the dining-room, and reached a chair just as Lisa replaced the receiver.

'Who was it, darling?'

Lisa's eyes grew wide with concern as she looked across at her mother. 'It was Matt. He's going to come and see if you're all right.' Two big tears spilled over and coursed down her cheeks as she ran to Karen's side. 'You won't have to go to hospital, will you?'

It would have to be Matt, wouldn't it, Karen groaned silently. Just when she'd conditioned herself into think-

ing she'd never see him again, he had to reappear at
what could hardly be termed a propitious moment!
'No, I don't think so,' she assured Lisa as the little
girl's lips began to tremble.

'I didn't know if you could get up, and I wouldn't
have been able to lift you. I had to tell somebody,'
Lisa burst out.

'Hush, honey,' Karen consoled gently. 'I've only
suffered a few bruises.' The poor little mite looked
white with anxiety. 'Be an angel and put tokens in
three empty bottles, then take them out to the gate
for the milkman.' If she gave her a few chores to do, it
would take her mind off things. 'And after that you
can call Tiddles—he usually has some milk around
this time, doesn't he?'

Lisa seemed reluctant to move away, and Karen had
to gently urge her to hurry so that the tasks would
be completed before Matt arrived.

His expression when he walked into the dining-room
some ten minutes later was hard to discern, and Karen
hastened to make light of the incident.

'I'm sorry if Lisa gave you a distorted version of
what happened,' she began calmly. 'I'm really fine.' Her
heartbeat quickened alarmingly as she looked up and
met his gaze, for he appeared every bit as compelling
as she remembered.

Matt's eyes swept over her, his appraisal swift and
analytical. 'Perhaps you'll allow me to judge that for
myself. Did you hit your head when you fell?'

'No—so I won't suffer from delayed concussion.'
She looked up at him with faint alarm as he crossed
the room to stand less than a foot away. 'I'll have a few
bruises tomorrow,' she essayed with a slight shrug that
ended in a wince of pain, and his eyes narrowed.

'Your shoulder? Did you knock it against anything?'

'The bath tub. I've jarred it, that's all,' she said defensively.

'Judging by your pallor, I'd say you've done more than that,' Matt determined bluntly. 'Who's your doctor?'

'Oh, really!' Karen derided crossly.

'Do as you're told,' he advised quietly. 'Now, what's his number?'

Karen shot him a look that would have withered a lesser man, before capitulating with a sigh of resignation. If she didn't he'd just as likely put her in his car and drive to the nearest hospital.

The surgery was almost empty when they arrived, and they were shown in to the doctor some fifteen minutes later. The fact that Matt accompanied her irked Karen unreasonably, and all through the doctor's examination she was aware of him beyond the screen listening to everything that was said as if he had the right to be there. Fortunately it was nothing more serious than a dislocated shoulder, which the doctor manipulated, then he supported her arm in a sling.

'Well, my dear, that shoulder will be painful for a few days. Stretched ligaments and contusions,' he explained. 'Rest, and keep it supported until Monday or Tuesday, then treat it with extreme care for a further week. Contact me if it gives you any trouble.'

The drive back to the house was achieved in almost total silence, and the minute the car whispered to a halt Karen issued a polite little speech of thanks, then slid out as quickly as her injuries would allow.

'Take the keys from my bag, there's a good girl,' she bade Lisa as they mounted the few steps to the

front porch, and then gave a start of surprise at Matt
stepped ahead and unlocked the door.

'Tell me where you keep your suitcases, and I'll
get one down,' he directed with ease as he entered the
house ahead of them, and when Karen looked at him in
askance, he merely smiled. 'You're coming back with
me until that arm is mobile.'

'I am not! I can manage——'

'You won't be able to drive a car for at least three
or four days,' he interrupted smoothly. 'How do you
propose to get Lisa to school? Household chores will
be difficult, even with her help. It will be much simpler
if you both move into my house and allow Mrs Rogers
to give whatever assistance is necessary for a few days.'

'Thank you, but we'll manage,' Karen insisted stoically, and saw his eyes darken fractionally.

'My dear Karen,' he began mildly, 'anyone would
think I had designs on your virtue.'

'Haven't you?'

His steady gaze unnerved her, and after a few seconds
she had to look away. 'You have no right to order me
about,' she said crossly as she walked down the hallway towards her bedroom.

'We'll discuss that later,' Matt drawled. 'Now, I'm
more concerned with getting you home.'

'I am home,' she snapped.

'As irksome as you find accepting my hospitality,' he
declared sardonically, 'you'd be advised to regard it as
a necessary expedient. The other alternative is to contact your mother and ask her to come down for a week,
as I have no intention of allowing you to stay here
alone. Which is it to be?'

Stupid tears clouded her vision. He was being con-
siderate of her welfare, yet all she could do was show

a childlike belligerence. 'There are some suitcases in
that cupboard above the wardrobe,' she indicated
huskily. 'I'll get some clothes together.'

'Tell me which drawers need opening.'

'I can do that myself.'

'With one hand?' Matt queried cynically, and she
choked angrily,

'I'm not completely helpless!'

'Stop it, Karen,' he advised softly. 'It won't do for
Lisa to discover us quarrelling.'

She flung him a dark look. 'If you weren't so objec-
tionably overbearing——'

'Pack some clothes,' he commanded brusquely. 'I'll
get Lisa to do likewise. Call me if you need any help.'

Oh, he was impossible! Crossly, she flung a selection
of undergarments, night attire, some skirts and jum-
pers into the suitcase he'd left open on the bed, then
she added a dress that buttoned to the waist and a cardigan. A few other sundry items, and her packing was
completed.

Lisa, the little imp, was delighted with the prospect
of staying in Matt's home, and together with Tiddles
firmly secure in his cat-basket on the rear seat of the
Jaguar, they drove through the Orakei basin towards
Kohimarama.

Karen felt a strange sense of trepidation as they
drew to a halt outside the large double-storied mansion.
She wasn't equipped to deal with several days spent
in Matt's company, or the evenings. She must be mad
to even contemplate it!

'I'll ring Grace this evening,' she murmured on a
slightly desperate note. 'Then it will only be necessary to inconvenience you for one night.'

'It's no inconvenience, Karen,' Matt drawled quietly,

turning towards her. 'It's a large house, and Mrs Rogers will be delighted to have some feminine company for a change.'

'It's very good of you,' she murmured politely, good manners surfacing, and he gave a soft chuckle.

'Relax, Karen,' he mocked gently. 'I shan't eat you for supper—or breakfast.'

'I wouldn't allow you to,' she retorted stiffly, mortified as a blush warmed her cheeks.

'Let's go inside, shall we?' Matt suggested blandly. 'I for one could do with a drink.'

As they moved through the main entrance foyer the housekeeper came forward to greet them, and her faintly shocked expression drew Karen's attention to her attire.

'Oh, my dear, what have you done?'

Lord, she must look a sight! Faded jeans, an over-large jumper that had seen better days, and both spotted with paint! She probably had paint on her face as well.

'My blood chills at the very thought,' Matt declared dryly. 'Suffice it to say Karen's the worse for wear after losing a battle with the bathtub—in which she was precariously perched on a chair while attempting to paint the ceiling.' He glanced down at Karen, then smiled as he leant out an idle finger and touched the tip of her nose. 'She needs help to shed her clothes. I'd offer my assistance, but I doubt it would be appreciated.' His gaze shifted to Lisa, and he offered her his hand. 'Come on, infant,' he bade with a smile. 'I'll take you upstairs and show you which room you'll be sleeping in. Then together we'll acquaint Tiddles with his new surroundings.'

CHAPTER SEVEN

WITH Mrs Rogers' help, Karen undressed and took a shower, then she changed into a button-through shirt-waister dress and slipped a cardigan around her shoulders. The pain-killing tablets the doctor had prescribed were beginning to take effect, reducing her shoulder and arm to a dull throbbing ache.

'Do you think you can manage now?'

Karen turned slightly and gave the kindly woman a smile. 'Yes, I'll be fine. Thanks for your help.'

'Rest for a while, and come downstairs when you're ready. Dinner will be served at six-thirty.'

'I'd better check where Lisa is,' Karen began with a slight frown, only to see the other woman wave a dismissing hand.

'She'll be with Matt,' Mrs Rogers determined calmly. 'He'll entertain her until dinner.'

'I'll just run a comb through my hair, then I'll look for her,' Karen declared. 'I'd hate her to make a nuisance of herself.'

'She appears to be a delightful little girl, I'm sure she wouldn't do that,' the other woman demurred as she crossed the room and paused beside the door. 'I'll be downstairs in the kitchen if you should need me for anything.'

Karen made a polite rejoinder, then turned to regard the room she'd been given. It was delightfully feminine, with flounced chintz curtains at the windows, white vinyl paper patterned with tiny flower sprigs adorning the walls, and colonial-style furniture. It had an adjoining bathroom, and Lisa occupied a similar suite opposite.

Idly she crossed to the window and looked out. Even the encroaching dusk failed to disguise the well-tended lawns and shrubs, the stand of mature trees that concealed neighbouring properties, thus gaining seclusion. The house stood on high ground and commanded a panoramic view of the harbour, from St Heliers sweeping several miles round the bay to encompass the complexity of wharves at the base of downtown Auckland. Street lights were springing on in groups, and within minutes they provided a delicate tracery of tiny lights, which from this distance resembled a fairyland by night.

'I did knock, but you're obviously lost in thought,' a familiar voice drawled from behind, and Karen turned to search Matt's features in the semi-darkness.

'It's this view,' she explained. 'I can't imagine anyone ever tiring of looking at it—especially at night. It's beautiful,' she ended simply.

'Yes, isn't it,' Matt agreed, his eyes on her upturned face. Idly he leant out a hand to tuck a stray lock of her hair back behind her ear. 'How's the shoulder?'

'Not too bad,' she answered cautiously. 'Where's Lisa?'

'Watching television. I thought you might like to come downstairs for a drink. Dinner will be ready soon.'

Karen blinked. It couldn't be after six, surely? 'I'm sorry,' she murmured. 'I didn't realise it was so late.'

'There's no need to apologise, Karen. Shall we go?'

She preceded him from the room, and was conscious of his close proximity as they moved along the hallway and descended the wide staircase.

Lisa sat curled up on the floor in the far corner of

the lounge, her eyes intent on the television screen, and apart from a quick smile at her mother when Karen entered the room with Matt, she remained glued to the programme until it was time to go in to dinner.

The meal comprised three courses, and Karen was able to consume the minestrone without any difficulty. However, when it came to the main dish, she was forced to allow Matt to place a selection of food on to her plate from various serving-dishes, and had to suffer the added indignity of having him cut her meat into bite-size portions.

It was a relief to leave the dining-room after dessert was served, and she chose a chair in the lounge as far away from his disturbing presence as possible. All through dinner she'd been aware of him to a startling degree, and now all she wanted to do was escape.

'If you don't mind, I'll have an early night,' Karen excused with polite civility, fixing her attention on the knotted silk tie at the base of Matt's throat. 'Lisa may be restless, sleeping in a strange room, and I'd prefer to be within earshot in case she wakes.' She stood to her feet and caught hold of her daughter's hand, then together they began walking towards the door.

Matt inclined his head, then moved to escort them from the room.

'Goodnight, Matt,' the little girl bade him engagingly. 'Can I kiss you?'

Oh lord, Karen groaned, watching as Matt scooped Lisa up against his chest and gave her a bear-like hug. To her amazement Lisa flung her arms around his neck and kissed his cheek.

'Goodnight, imp,' he grinned, lowering her to the floor. 'Sleep well.' The look he directed Karen was sardonic, and there was a wry twinkle in those tawny depths—almost, she decided, as if he intended to kiss her goodnight, as well.

With considerable aplomb she beat a rapid retreat, and didn't breathe easily until she reached the upper floor.

Lisa washed fastidiously, then donned her nightgown and hopped into bed, wriggling into a comfortable position as Karen began a bedtime story.

Within ten minutes the little tot's eyes were closed, her breathing steady, and cautiously Karen left the room. She closed the door gently behind her, and turned to cross the hallway to her own room, only to come to an abrupt halt at the sight of Matt leaning indolently against the door-jamb.

He held up a bottle of tablets. 'You forgot to take these,' he indicated quietly. 'I imagine you'll need them to get through the night without suffering unnecessary discomfort.'

She swallowed compulsively. 'Thank you.'

Matt opened the door to her room and switched on the light. 'Ann and Ben Rogers have retired to their quarters for the night,' he informed her, his expression becoming wry as he noticed her apprehension. 'Do you need any help to undress?'

'No,' she denied hastily. 'I'll manage—thank you.'

'If your bra has a back fastening, I doubt you will,' he declared dryly, and she gasped out loud,

'You don't mean to tell me you intend playing lady's maid?'

'Unfastening your bra, Karen—not undressing you. There is a difference between the two. Not,' he added sardonically, 'that the latter wouldn't afford me considerable pleasure in more—suitable circumstances.' He noted her angry blush with wry amusement. 'If you'll undo those buttons,' he directed gently, 'I'll unclip the offending garment, then discreetly disappear.' When she didn't move, he added quietly, 'Relax, Karen. Seducing an injured female isn't my style.'

She stood rooted to the spot as he moved towards her, and when his fingers touched the uppermost button on her dress she took a backward step. 'Please don't. I can manage.'

Matt gazed at her steadily, then calmly reached out and began undoing the buttons, unbuckled the belt at her waist, and, turning her firmly away from him, he eased the dress carefully from her shoulders and unfastened the clip of her bra.

Karen let out the breath she'd been unconsciously holding over the past few seconds. Her skin tingled where his fingers had touched, albeit impersonally, and she couldn't have uttered a word if her life had depended on it.

'That wasn't such an ordeal, was it?' his voice drawled from behind, and lifting a handful of her hair, he bestowed a lingering kiss to her nape. 'I'm at the far end of the hall, if you should need anything through the night. Sleep well, Karen.'

The instant she heard the door click shut, she collapsed into a shaky heap on the bed, and it was several minutes before she extracted a nightgown and made for the bathroom. Only being able to use one hand made for awkwardness, but she managed to divest the remainder of her clothes and slip into her nightgown without too much difficulty. Filling a glass with water, she extracted two tablets and took them, then refilled the glass and carried it through to the bedroom and placed it on the small bedside table in readiness should she need it during the night.

A few hours later she lay awake, unable to sleep. Reaching out, she switched on the bedside lamp and checked her wristwatch, discovering to her dismay that it was the lighter side of midnight. If only she'd brought a book to read—even a magazine would do. Perhaps she could check that Lisa was all right, then she could make her way downstairs to the lounge where there was a bookcase filled with books. She didn't imagine Matt would object if she borrowed one or two.

Slipping out of bed, she managed to put a wrap around her shoulders, then she emerged from the room and crossed the hall to discover that Lisa was sound asleep. Quietly she closed the door, and made her way to the head of the stairs. Stepping cautiously, she reached the lower floor, then stifled a groan of dismay as she realised she had no idea where the light switches were located. The flood of light from her bedroom had provided sufficient illumination upstairs, but the lower floor was swathed in darkness, and she didn't relish stumbling into objects she couldn't see. There was little else she could do but return to her room, and with a sigh she began mounting the stairs.

The sound of a door opening and the sudden stream of light startled her momentarily, and she stood in frozen silence as Matt's robed figure came into view.

'Having trouble getting to sleep?'

'I—yes,' she stammered. 'I'm sorry if I disturbed you. I thought if I had something to read—I remembered seeing some books in the lounge, but when I got downstairs I couldn't find a light switch.'

Matt's lips moved into a faintly quizzical smile. 'I wasn't asleep. Would you like some hot milk?'

It sounded a tempting offer. 'If you'll show me where the kitchen is, I'll make it.'

'Go back to bed, Karen. It will take only a few minutes.'

She longed to argue with him, but instinct warned it would be wiser to do as she was told, and with a murmured word of thanks she continued up the stairs.

The sheets were modestly arranged to cover her from the neck down when Matt entered the bedroom, and one eyebrow rose in amusement as he placed the mug of steaming milk down beside her. In his other hand he held no fewer than four books and a few magazines.

'I'm not familiar with your reading tastes, but you should find something there to hold your interest.' His gaze took in her pallor, the vivid blue eyes wide and hauntingly dark, 'Is that shoulder giving you much pain?'

'It's not too bad,' Karen answered cautiously, willing him to go. An intimacy had crept into the room, unbidden, and she had the wildest longing to be kissed—which was madness.

'Sip your milk,' Matt commanded gently, handing her the mug, and she obediently took a mouthful.

'What did you put in this?'

'A dash of brandy—it will help you sleep.'

She wrinkled her nose at him. 'A very liberal dash, judging by the taste of it. If I drink all of this, I'll become inebriated!'

He smiled, and his eyes gleamed with humour. 'I very much doubt it. To do that, it would take more than one measure of brandy I added. Now, drink it slowly—all of it. Then I'll leave you to read for a while.'

'Yes, sir.'

'You're hardly in a position to proffer any sassy remarks,' he chided, his smile faintly sardonic.

'I'm safe from any advances—you said as much,' she parried, looking at him over the rim of the mug. The brandy was beginning to have the strangest effect, and she felt deliciously warm and light-headed—almost as if she was floating on a lovely soft cloud.

'Hmm,' Matt considered thoughtfully. 'I think you've had enough.' He took the mug from her hand and drained the contents, then he leaned forward and brushed his lips against her temple. 'Sweet dreams.'

She felt oddly reluctant to be left alone. 'I haven't thanked you for rescuing me,' she began in a rush. 'Or for the hospitality you've extended.'

He looked down at her steadily, and for an instant there was a flaring of emotion in those dark tawny eyes, then it was gone and she was left to wonder if it had been a figment of her imagination.

'It's very kind of you,' she added, and glimpsed his wry smile.

'You can thank me properly at a more appropriate time. However, this will have to suffice for the present.' He lowered his head and placed his mouth on hers, moving his lips gently in a soft butterfly kiss.

Of their own volition her lips parted, and she sensed rather than heard his indrawn breath, then he was kissing her with a sensual mastery that brought alive a deep physical ache within, until she became a mindless, floating entity beneath his touch.

With lingering regret he raised his head, and his eyes were dark with tightly-controlled passion. 'If I stay here much longer, I won't be answerable for the consequences—and in your present state, it would be taking an unfair advantage.' He bent and bruised her mouth with a brief, hard kiss, then straightening, he turned and walked from the room.

Karen gave a deep shuddering sigh, then sorted through the books with a decidedly shaky hand. Trying to concentrate on the printed text proved hopeless, for the words became blurred and failed to make any sense, and after a while she reached out and switched off the lamp.

The memory of Matt's kisses remained with her in the darkness, and when she lapsed into sleep his image returned to haunt her dreams, becoming inextricably interwoven with a sinister image of Brad, until it became impossible to distinguish between the two.

Saturday dawned bright and clear, and Karen awoke to the sound of curtains being drawn. The faint aroma of coffee was tantalising, and glancing towards its source she espied a tray resting on the bedside table with no fewer than two covered dishes, a rack containing toast, coffee, and an interesting assortment of spreads—honey, marmalade, and raspberry conserve.

'Can you manage to sit up, my dear?' Mrs Rogers queried kindly, her expression wreathed with concern. 'Matt suggested a tray, rather than have you come down for breakfast. I've let you sleep in, as no doubt you had a disturbed night.'

Karen eased herself up against the pillows and pushed the hair away from her face. 'What is the time—Lisa——?'

'It's almost nine-thirty,' the other woman told her gently. 'And Lisa is fine. She had breakfast with Matt two hours ago, and since then she's been helping me. She'll be in to see you any second now.'

The next instant Lisa burst into the room, her small

face bright with laughter. 'Mummy! You've been asleep so long.' She stopped beside the bed and regarded Karen anxiously. 'Is your shoulder very bad?' Excitement sparkled in her eyes as she announced, 'Matt's gone to golf, but he's coming back for lunch, then he's going to take me and Jeremy to the cinema this afternoon. And tomorrow, if it's fine, we're all going to Helensville for a swim and a barbecue tea. Matt said Jeremy can come, too.' She paused for breath, then broke into another spate of excited speech. 'Matt's got a dog—he's big, bigger than me—and he's called Barnaby. And Mrs Rogers has got a cat that's white with big splotches of ginger and brown and black all over it—just like the guinea-pigs at school. Tiddles doesn't like him, but he likes Barnaby. Can I have a piece of your toast?'

Karen caught Mrs Roger's eye, and tried to conceal her amusement. 'Yes,' she answered solemnly. 'Then when I've finished breakfast, you can help me get dressed.'

An hour later Karen allowed herself to be led outside to inspect the grounds, and to be introduced to the much-discussed Barnaby. Huge, he undoubtedly was, being a breed of Old English Sheepdog, and he was positively adorable. He bounded about, running in circles around Lisa, then he sat back on his haunches, his pink tongue lolling as he panted from the exertion.

'Oh, you beautiful thing!' Karen cried softly, leaning out a hand to fondle his head, and his tail thumped in silent appreciation.

'He's gorgeous,' Lisa enthused with obvious affection. 'Matt says he's just an overgrown bundle of hair who eats enough food a day to keep a whole family alive.' She pointed towards the high fence bounding the grounds. 'Look at that lovely tree, with all those leaves and funny little twisted branches.'

The willow trailed its weeping twig-like branches almost to the ground, and was ideally situated in the corner, its trunk surrounded by an ornate pebble-garden. The spacious lawns were well cared for, the edges neatly clipped, and Karen could only conclude that keeping them in order must be Ben's responsibility.

'Look—there's Matt now, and he's got Jeremy with him.'

Karen glanced towards the drive and saw the long sleek Jaguar glide to a smooth halt on the paved area adjoining the main entrance. Her footsteps slowed as Lisa broke into a run, and she watched Matt emerge from the car to sweep the little girl high into the air the instant Lisa flung herself into his arms. She could hear their laughter together with the children's excited chatter as they waited for her to join them.

Matt's scrutiny was swift and analytical. 'How do you feel?' He turned briefly to admonish the exuberant Barnaby, then returned his attention to Karen. 'Is the shoulder any worse?'

'I'm fine,' she responded evenly, although there was nothing even about the way her pulse began to race at the sight of him. Dressed casually in grey suede trousers and a navy shirt, he exuded a raw masculinity that bothered her more than she cared to admit.

'Hmm,' he commented dryly. 'At a guess, that shoulder has stiffened up, and your left side is one continuous ache. Did you sleep well?'

'Yes, thank you.' Lord, she sounded like a polite little schoolgirl! For the sake of something to say, she stumbled into speech. 'Lisa tells me you intend taking both her and Jeremy to the cinema this afternoon. It's very kind of you to entertain her.'

'She's a delightful child,' Matt answered quietly. 'Shall we go inside? Perhaps you'd like a glass of sherry before lunch?'

'Lunch?' Karen managed with a shaky laugh. 'I've not long finished breakfast!'

However, she did justice to a bowl of delicious soup, and sat back while the others ate cold meat and salad, followed by fresh fruit.

The large house seemed unusually quiet after Matt had departed for the city with Lisa and Jeremy, and Karen settled herself comfortably in the lounge to read. Her shoulder felt stiff, and the slightest movement caused it to throb painfully—what was more, her leg and hip felt bruised and sore, indicating that her shoulder and arm hadn't entirely taken the brunt of her fall.

Matt returned with Lisa and Jeremy shortly before five, and the two children were obviously enthralled by the film they had seen—an inter-galactic extravaganza that had received several nominations and awards for its special effects.

Dinner wasn't the ordeal Karen expected it to be, for the children's presence ensured there was no lull in the conversation, and Mrs Rogers served a delicious casserole which Karen was able to eat unaided by any help from Matt.

Both children were permitted to have their bedtime extended by an hour, and Karen couldn't conceal her surprise when Matt declared he would supervise his nephew into bed. He seemed far removed from any paternal image, yet it was clear he was held in high regard.

Lisa opted to regale Karen with vivid details of the film she'd seen that afternoon, thus eliminating the usual bedtime story, and it wasn't long before the little girl fell into an exhausted sleep. She looked angelic, her flaxen hair plaited to prevent any tangles while she slept, her lashes long and contrastingly dark—the only visual resemblance she bore to Brad, who had been as dark as Karen was fair.

As Karen closed the door quietly behind her, she turned and saw Matt standing in the hallway.

'I'll take a look at that shoulder,' he indicated without preamble, and Karen gasped an angry retort, only to have it brushed aside. 'It's obvious that it's giving you considerable pain, and besides, that sling needs adjusting,' he declared evenly, then he went on in a voice that had become dangerously soft, 'Don't say you can manage to do it yourself, Karen.'

She threw him a look that had no effect whatever, and entered her room with a feeling of angry resignation. 'You're being insufferably bossy,' she ventured tightly, and stood in the centre of the room as he removed the sling. Her eyes flared brightly as he began undoing the buttons on her dress, and angry tears welled up and threatened to spill down her cheeks as he eased the garment off to leave her standing in a bra and slip.

'Is the pain any worse than it was yesterday?' His glance speared her mercilessly. 'No polite fabrications this time, Karen. It's important.'

'I didn't expect it to get better overnight.'

'No,' Matt conceded. 'But the pain shouldn't be so severe that it leaves you white-faced and hollow-eyed.' His eyes narrowed fractionally as he assisted her into the dress, then he replaced the sling. 'I'm of the opinion the shoulder should be X-rayed. It's possible there's a pinched nerve. I'll telephone the doctor, then take you to hospital.'

'Now?' she queried incredulously. 'What about the children?'

'They're both asleep, but I'll arrange for Ann Rogers to stay in the house while we're away.'

'I think you're making an unnecessary fuss,' she declared with something akin to angry frustration. 'I could refuse to accede to such blatant highhandedness ...' she trailed off expressively. 'You can't *make* me go to hospital.'

'You can walk to the car—or I carry you,' he averred brusquely. 'It's immaterial, either way.'

'I hate you,' Karen whispered, and could cheerfully have hit him at that precise moment.

'Which is it to be?' He slipped an arm around her waist and leant down to place the other behind her knees, then he lifted her as effortlessly as if she weighed little more than a child.

'Put me down!' she flung furiously. 'I'll walk!'

The next few hours were a blur. There was the inevitable wait at the hospital, followed by X-rays, consultation with the doctor, then manipulation, further X-rays, until Karen thought it would never end. Finally she was pronounced free to leave, and although her shoulder hurt, the pain was less intense.

All the way home she battled with the right words to thank Matt, but when the car drew to a halt in the courtyard outside his palatial residence, she hadn't uttered one of them.

The children were reported not to have stirred, and after murmuring an indistinct 'goodnight', Karen made her way up the stairs to her room.

She was almost in bed when the door opened after the briefest knock, and she coloured deeply beneath Matt's penetrating gaze, conscious of her nightgown and the way it clung to her slender curves.

'I've managed without your help to discard my clothes,' she choked resentfully. 'I've taken two tablets, as prescribed, and now I'd like to go to sleep.'

'In that case, I'll bid you goodnight,' he declared silkily, retracing his steps and closing the door quietly behind him.

Karen grimaced, her eyes clouding with remorse. He'd looked ready to shake her, and the realisation that she deserved it didn't help at all.

The following day Matt took Karen, together with Lisa and Jeremy, to the heated pool in the Parakai reserve at Helensville. They left after an early lunch, and stowed in the boot of the Jaguar was a portable barbecue and a hamper packed with food.

Karen contented herself with watching the children frolic and swim in the pool, and after a brief glance at Matt attired in swimming briefs, she endeavoured to look anywhere but at him. His physique was superb, a well-muscled frame that behoved physical fitness. He looked strong and utterly male, and while one half of her wanted to become part of him, the other wanted to run and hide.

He treated Lisa with an indolent charm and distributed his affection equally between the two children, and after they'd changed back into warm clothes he led them each by the hand to the park immediately adjacent to the thermal pool.

It was a relaxed, carefree afternoon, and after an early meal of barbecued sausages and steak, salad and fruit, they packed everything into the Jaguar and drove back to the city, pausing briefly on the way so that Lisa and Jeremy could see the various cargo ships in port. Then Matt deposited his nephew with Janine, and refused his sister's invitation to stay for coffee on the grounds that Karen was tired—which angered Karen considerably, for although she *was*, she considered his proprietorial manner extremely irksome.

Therefore, on arriving home, it gave her the utmost pleasure to refuse, albeit politely, his offer to return downstairs after putting Lisa to bed. Although the dark sardonic gleam she glimpsed in his eyes destroyed any satisfaction she achieved by refusing. He was all too aware of the reason behind her refusal, and the fact that he found it amusing was galling.

At what time Karen woke she had no idea, for the room was in darkness. Rather shakily she reached out and switched on the bedside lamp, blinking against the sudden light as she attempted to orientate herself with her surroundings. The black nightmarish void from which she'd just emerged was a haunting, vivid memory, and she forced herself to breath deeply and evenly in an effort to calm her madly-racing heart.

Oh dear God, she groaned in despair. Not again. Please, not here—especially not here. If she'd cried out——

The bedroom door opened without warning and Matt stood in its aperture, his expression a curious mixture of anger and concern, and in that instant she knew the voice she'd heard in her nightmare had been her own.

'I'm all right,' she offered hesitantly. 'I'm—sorry if I woke you——'

'I'll get you some brandy,' Matt declared quietly, and

his eyes darkened as they followed the shaky movement of her hand as it pushed back a few tendrils of hair.

'No,' she refused quickly, unaware of the way her eyes clung to him, pleading with him not to leave her alone.

'A hot drink?'

Karen shook her head. 'No. I—don't——' she stammered despairingly. 'Please—don't go.' To her horror one solitary tear spilled over and ran slowly down her cheek, to be followed by another, and another. What a fool she must be making of herself, she derided silently, but was unable to control the flow. A handkerchief proved elusive, and she gave a start when the side of the bed depressed and a large linen square was tucked into her hand.

'Do you want to talk about it?' he queried gently, and Karen considered the question carefully, then slowly shook her head.

What could she say? If she began, she'd have to tell him the whole sordid story, and the last thing she wanted from him was pity—anything but that.

'Do these nightmares happen frequently?' Matt probed, his expression an enigmatic mask. Idly he leant out an arm and drew her head against his shoulder.

'Not—usually,' she murmured, feeling strangely safe and secure. She could have closed her eyes, and resting against him, slipped into sleep. For one crazy moment she wished she could, then common sense prevailed, and rather reluctantly she stirred. 'I'll be all right now.' She tried to raise her head, and found she couldn't. 'Please, Matt.'

With that, he shifted his weight slightly so that she could slip down between the sheets, and when her head lay against the pillow he leant down and wound a lock of flaxen hair between his fingers.

'This is like silk,' he said musingly, then with a slight smile he released it and stood to his feet. 'Impossible to imagine I'm tucking in a child,' he smiled as he pulled the covers into place. 'My instincts where you are concerned are far from paternal.' He leant down and brushed his lips against her forehead, then trailed gentle fingers down her cheek. 'Close your eyes, Karen. I'll stay with you until you fall asleep.'

With a small sigh Karen did as she was told, and as unlikely as she thought it would be for her to fall asleep with Matt in the room, she eventually did lapse into that somnolent state, and her dreams weren't plagued with fearful images.

At some later stage she must have stirred, for she became aware that the bedside lamp was still switched on, and half asleep, she reached up to turn it off. A slight movement beside her arrested her hand in mid-air, and she cast a startled glance towards the cause and saw Matt's long frame stretched out beside her.

Cautiously she raised her head, then gave a sound-less gasp as she realised a length of her hair had become imprisoned on the pillow beneath his head. Oh lord, now what? she groaned. One thing was certain. She had to wake him.

A touch on his arm, perhaps—and if she quietly called his name——

In that instant his eyelids swept open and she found herself gazing into a pair of tawny-gold eyes that held a frightening awareness. A slow smile pulled at the edges of his mouth, and using an elbow to support his head he shifted his weight and turned towards her.

His hand moved slowly to trace the outline of her mouth, and the feather-soft touch was strangely evocative, so that she was powerless to move away or offer any protest as he lowered his head.

His mouth closed over hers warmly, teasing gently at first, then becoming disruptively sensual as he probed the sweet moistness within. A shaft of exquisite pleasure shot through her body as his hand slid down her throat to the thin silk encasing her breasts, and a soft moan escaped her as his lips trailed a similar path.

It was only when she felt his hand slide down over her stomach that sanity returned, and with it came a sense of shame, a growing horror, as what was happening between them.

'Matt—no!' she gasped shakily, the familiar fear rising inside her like an all-encompassing nausea, making her breathing ragged, her eyes wide with fright.

'Karen—in the name of heaven,' he groaned, and his mouth travelled up to settle on hers with a seducing quality that was difficult to ignore.

With renewed strength Karen twisted her head, managing at last to free her mouth, and she lay there trembling, shocked at what she had unwittingly invited.

'I'm sorry,' she whispered interminable seconds later, and she gasped as firm fingers grasped her chin and forced her to look at him.

'Not nearly as sorry as I am,' Matt evinced regretfully, his eyes dark with passion.

'I didn't mean——' she stammered haltingly, then stumbled on, 'I should never have asked you to—stay.'

His smile was fleeting. 'The blame can be equally attributed,' he shrugged wryly. 'I take it you want me to leave?'

Karen didn't trust herself to speak, and after what

seemed an age he slid off the bed and stood to his feet.

The look he cast her was impossible to discern as he raked a hand through his hair, ruffling it into a state of unruliness. 'I'm not accustomed to taking a cold shower at any time of the night—or day,' he relayed dryly, looking down at her with a measure of cynical amusement. 'But since knowing you, it's becoming something of a habit.' He bent down and bestowed a brief hard kiss to her lips, then he turned and left the room.

For a long time she lay still, powerless to move, as she attempted to gather her jangling nerves into something resembling normalcy. Dear God—how could she ever face him again?

Sleep was never more difficult to summon, and she lay there staring into the darkness until an early dawn began filtering through the drapes.

CHAPTER EIGHT

'I'll be leaving just as soon as Ben brings Lisa back from school this afternoon,' Karen declared firmly, and saw Mrs Rogers' look of consternation. 'He won't mind driving us home immediately afterwards, will he?'

'No, of course not,' the housekeeper concurred, clearly perplexed. 'But don't you think you should stay a little longer—at least until Matt arrives home this evening?'

'No, that won't be necessary,' Karen declined with a polite smile. 'My shoulder is much better, and staying here was only meant to be a very temporary thing. It's been very kind of—Matt to take us under his wing. And I'd like to thank you, too, for looking after us,' she added courteously.

'Thank you, dear,' Mrs Rogers accepted, shooting Karen a thoughtful glance. 'But Matt frequently has guests to stay—looking after them is part of my job.'

That had interesting connotations she didn't dare contemplate. 'I'll go upstairs and finish packing,' she said hurriedly. 'Then there'll be no need to delay Ben unnecessarily. It's almost two o'clock, now.'

'Karen, don't you think you should stay? At least until Matt returns this evening?' the older woman queried placatingly, and Karen shook her head.

'No,' she declared swiftly, unable to meet the other's concerned gaze. How could she say that it was impossible for her to stay after last night? She'd remained upstairs fussing unnecessarily over her own and Lisa's toilette until she was sure that Matt had left for work, and she couldn't bear to be here when he arrived home. She *had* to leave.

Fortunately Lisa accepted the rather glib explanation Karen offered, and with Tiddles ensconced in his cat-basket, the trio were competently driven by a vaguely disapproving Ben to their endearingly familiar house in Remuera.

Karen deliberately refrained from contemplating what Matt's reaction would be when he discovered she'd returned home. He could think what he liked, for nothing could persuade her to spend another night beneath his roof. Remembering how it felt to lie close beside him for several hours caused a wave of embarrassment that was difficult to ignore.

Soon after Ben departed, she completed a few necessary chores with Lisa's help, then she set about preparing their evening meal.

At seven-thirty she tucked the little girl into bed and tiptoed quietly from the room. In the lounge she changed television channels and tried to summon an interest in the comedy series projected on the screen, only to find her attention wandering at all too-frequent intervals.

Oh, this was no good at all, she decided crossly. She might as well have a shower and go to bed. An early night with an absorbing book was better than sitting here alone and slipping into a mood of introspection.

The warm needle-spray proved relaxing, and Karen turned the dial up a fraction, enjoying the luxury of hot water cascading over her body for a few more minutes before closing off the taps. She completed her toilette and was about to slip a robe over her nightgown when there were several staccato raps on the front door.

There was only one person it could be, and by the

time she reached the end of the hallway she was a mass of nerves.

'Who is it?' she queried cautiously.

'Matt, Karen. Open the door.' His voice sounded inflexible, although his expression as he surveyed her was deliberately bland. 'Aren't you going to ask me in?'

Karen pulled the edges of her robe closer together in a gesture that was purely defensive. 'I—just got out from the shower. I intended going to bed,' she rushed heedlessly, opening the door further to allow him entry. In the confined space of the hallway he seemed much taller and broader than she remembered, and she felt intimidated by his presence.

Matt's eyes narrowed slightly as he stood there silently regarding her, then he leaned forward and brushed his lips against her temple.

The action was totally unexpected and set up a familiar curling sensation in her stomach. She could smell the cologne of his aftershave, and feel the warmth of his breath stirring a few stray tendrils of her hair.

'What do you want?' she queried, and was unable to refrain from demanding desperately, 'Why did you come?'

'Why did you leave?' he countered quietly, and when she didn't answer he pulled her into his arms and held her lightly. 'Karen, Karen—what am I going to do with you, hmm?' His lips trailed down to caress first one closed eyelid, then the other. 'Did my spending most of the night—however innocently—in your bed frighten you so much that you had to run away?'

There was nothing she could say, and after a few minutes he lifted her chin and forced her to meet his gaze.

'I'm flying down to Christchurch tomorrow morning

for a series of business meetings that will take a few days. I'd feel a lot easier in my mind if you'd stay in my home where Ann Rogers can take care of you while I'm away.'

For a moment she faltered, for without his disturbing presence she would have enjoyed being his houseguest. 'Thank you for your concern,' she refused politely. 'But I'd prefer to remain here.'

'There is, of course, an alternative,' he drawled musingly. 'You could come with me.'

Her eyes darkened until they resembled deep blue sapphires. 'You're wasting your time, Matt. Why don't you go and exercise your charm on someone else?' she queried, and her eyes became diamond-bright with anger. 'I'm sure you won't experience any difficulty in finding an eager, amenable companion to accompany you. Berenice would doubtless jump at the chance.' Her laugh sounded faintly bitter. 'You're expert in the art of seduction—but I'm not that blind, or that gullible, to fall into your arms.'

Matt gave a silent shake of his head, then voiced wryly, 'You do leap to conclusions, don't you?'

'I'm adept at avoiding propositions.'

One eyebrow rose in cynical amusement, and he gave a soft mocking laugh. 'You should have let me finish.'

'A proposition is a proposition—no matter how you present it,' Karen accorded disparagingly.

'Even when it's legal?' His eyes gleamed quizzically, then darkened with controlled passion. 'Marriage, Karen. I want you waiting for me when I come home— in my bed all night long, to wake each morning in my arms.'

The colour drained from her face. 'You can't be serious,' she whispered at last.

His gaze was startlingly direct. 'Never more so, I assure you.'

Incredulity was evident in her voice as she proclaimed, 'But we've only known each other——'

'Three weeks,' he finished imperturbably.

'It's crazy,' she uttered shakily, and saw his lips curve into a gentle smile.

'You haunt me—always in my thoughts, invading my sleep. Your image is ever with me—day and night.' He leant out a hand and trailed his fingers down her cheek. 'No woman has been capable of that—until now.'

'I can't marry you.' There, she'd said it. But try as she might, she hadn't been able to keep the slight edge of panic from her voice.

'Would marriage to me be so terrible?' Matt queried lightly.

'I—have everything I need. A house, my own car,' she rushed desperately. 'I'm free to go where I please— I don't even have to work to support Lisa and myself. I only took a job to fill in time while Lisa was at school.'

'What do you think I'm going to do—lock you in a prison?'

Karen looked away, unable to hold his faintly teasing gaze any longer. 'You don't understand,' she said huskily.

'Try me.'

She felt torn between a need to explain and a loathing to lay bare the hurtful past. 'I can't marry you,' she said dully, and felt his fingers beneath her chin as he turned her face towards him.

'Are you still in love with him?'

'*No!*' she cried out, then ran her tongue along the edge of her lower lip in a purely nervous gesture. 'No,' she repeated slowly, and saw his eyes narrow.

'Then suppose you tell me why, Karen.'

Her head jerked back at that softly-voiced directive, anger uppermost in her emotions, to be replaced almost immediately by weary resignation.

'Oh, Matt,' she began helplessly, 'why can't you just accept——'

'I love you,' he declared quietly. 'Surely I'm entitled to some explanation.'

Karen's eyes dilated until they resembled huge pools, and she was incapable of uttering a word.

'I'm no inexperienced boy to be fooled by what we feel for each other,' Matt chided gently, and he gave her a slight shake. 'I want you, need you, in a way I never imagined I'd ever need any woman, and I refuse to believe that together we can't overcome whatever it is about marriage that frightens you so much.'

Suddenly her legs seemed unable to support her. 'I think we'd better go and sit down,' she decided shakily. 'Have you anything alcoholic to drink? I think we could both do with it.'

Seated in the lounge, Karen took a generous sip of sherry before setting the glass down on a nearby table, then she met his gaze with determined effort.

'I was a very young nineteen when I met Brad Ellman,' she began shakily. 'He was handsome and very charming, and in a matter of weeks he'd persuaded me to marry him.' A bitter laugh choked in her throat. 'He was very plausible, and like a silly little fool, I believed every word he said.' She swallowed painfully, then forced herself to continue. 'I had no idea I was merely a pawn in his diabolical scheme until four hours after the wedding. Apparently he'd been jilted an hour before he was due to walk down the aisle, and it had

taken him a year before he found a girl who bore a
close physical resemblance to his former fiancée. His
thirst for revenge was slaked by—raping me.'

Remembering caused a muscle to twitch nervously
along the edge of her jaw, and she had to force herself
to meet his eyes. 'When I—woke, some hours later, he
was gone.' She fell silent, then struggled to complete
the story. 'They found his car early next morning where
it had veered off the road and hurtled down into a deep
gorge. He was dead.'

She turned away and fixed her attention on a nearby
picture frame that adorned the wall. 'I changed my
name back to Ingalls, moved down to Auckland, and
secured a job. Then I discovered I was pregnant.' She
clasped her hands tightly together until the knuckles
showed white. 'I didn't want Brad's child, right up until it was born, and then she nearly died from a rare
complication which hadn't been aided by a premature
birth. Perhaps almost losing her made me want her to
live. She was mine—all mine,' she whispered softly.
'Even now, I refuse to concede that Lisa originated in
part from the man who was responsible for fathering
her.'

A silence seemed to fill the room for several minutes
after her voice trailed to a halt, then Matt demanded
gently,

'When will you marry me?'

Karen swung round to face him. 'Haven't I just explained?' she cried in anguish.

'You've explained one man's psycho-neurosis,' Matt
offered quietly. 'Something which only a mind men-
tally sick could dream up. You can't relegate me into a
similar role. The past is over, Karen.'

'Is it?' she queried dully. 'How do I know that what

you profess to feel for me isn't merely physical?'

He gave a wry smile. 'I don't have to dangle marriage as bait in front of any woman's nose to assuage my physical needs.'

'There's Lisa——'

Matt rebuked gently, 'Do you doubt my affection where she's concerned?'

'I need time to think,' Karen protested, faltering a little as he reached out a hand and touched her hair, then his lips brushed down her cheek towards the corner of her mouth to linger tantalisingly. 'Please, Matt. I——'

Whatever else she planned to say became locked in her throat as his lips covered hers, coaxing gently at first, then deepening into a passionate embrace that left her in no doubt of his desire.

A silent moan of entreaty escaped as his lips travelled down the pulsing cord at her neck to the opening of her robe, then made their provocative return to her mouth. A warmth invaded her lower limbs, then slowly spread over her entire body, and she clung to him un-ashamedly.

How long it was before he gently put her aside, she had no idea, and she sat within his encircling arms feeling totally bemused.

'As much as I'd like to stay, I think it would be wise for me to leave,' Matt declared huskily, and her bones seemed to melt beneath the warmth of his gaze. Gently he tilted her chin. 'I fly down to Christchurch early to-morrow morning.' He smiled softly. 'It's only fair to warn you that I don't intend to wait any longer than the necessary time it takes to get a licence.' He leant forward and bestowed a brief hard kiss on her mouth. 'I'll ring you tomorrow night from my hotel. Meantime, take care, sweet Karen. I've arranged for a contractor to come and complete the bathroom for you, so no more climbing ladders or stepping on to chairs, hmm?' He effectively stilled any protest she might have uttered, then stood to his feet.

The instant the Jaguar reversed down the drive Karen closed the front door, then returned to the lounge and sank down into a chair.

The events over the past hour had begun to take effect, and her mind rapidly assumed a state of turmoil. Even the thought of making herself some coffee seemed to involve too much effort.

She had to be mad to let another man's smooth talk and sensual expertise fool her—lulling her into a false sense of security. Because that was all it was—sensual expertise. It wasn't love—that was an all-encompassing emotion in which she no longer had any faith.

Three weeks—one didn't build a strong basis for any lasting relationship on the strength of so short an acquaintance.

They struck sparks off each other at every turn. What hope would they have, married to each other? And there wasn't only herself to consider—although Lisa adored him, and being an affectionate child she had easily been won over by Matt's undoubted charm.

But what of the intimacy marriage entailed? a tiny voice whispered inside her head. How would Matt react if she baulked at the initial sexual contact? It was an obstacle that began to assume cataclysmic proportion. All these years she'd pushed it to the back of her mind, certain that the situation would never arise. Now it rose like an angry monster to taunt her.

Lost in contemplative thought, it was a long time before Karen roused herself sufficiently to put off the lights and go to bed, and then sleep was an elusive captive, until finally she slipped from between the covers and shook out two tiny tablets from the bottle she kept in the medicine cabinet. Now she would be guaranteed several hours of merciful oblivion.

The after-effects of the sleeping pills made Karen feel lethargic, and she was almost tempted to go back to bed when she returned home after depositing Lisa at school. Having had breakfast she decided to have a cup of hot black coffee in the hope that it would revive her. She set about making it, then stirred in sugar and scanned through the daily newspaper as she drank it.

The thought of remaining on her own in the house all day was daunting, and with renewed determination she resolved to embark on a shopping expedition. Her shoulder was still stiff and sore, but it felt considerably better than it had the previous day.

There were several fashionable boutiques in Parnell Village, and Karen headed the car in that direction with the intention of spending an enjoyable day.

When she called to collect Lisa from school there were several packages reposing on the back seat, and her daughter's expressed pleasure at unwrapping the purchases brought a smile to her lips.

'We'll open them as soon as we get home,' Karen promised. 'Some are for you, and a few are for me. We can try them all on before I start preparing dinner.'

'I do love you, Mummy.'

Karen's heart turned over, and a lump rose in her throat. 'I love you, too, darling—very much.'

'When are we going to see Matt again?'

'He's away on business, honey.' She tried to keep her voice light. 'He'll be back in a few days.'

'I think he's awfully nice,' the little girl declared

earnestly. 'I liked staying in his house with Mrs Rogers and Ben. And Barnaby was fun to play with.'

'Even standing on all four legs, he was almost as tall as you,' Karen teased gently as she brought the Datsun to a halt in their driveway. 'Out, there's a good girl. I'll put the car away later.'

They spent the next hour unwrapping parcels and trying on clothes, deciding which accessories went best with each new garment. The delicate pink Swiss cotton with its tulle and lace petticoat was the perfect party frock for a five-year-old girl, and Lisa looked lovely in it. Karen's new dress was of printed *challis* in shades of pale apricot, beige, and light brown tonings on a dark background. Buttoned to the waist, it flared to mid-calf level in softly gathered folds, and had full batwing sleeves that were gathered in at each wrist. Added to her purchases were a pair of fashionable boots and matching handbag.

However, the most pleasing of her purchases were matching mother-and-daughter dresses that had been too eye-catching to resist.

She had just hung the last garment away when there was a knock at the door, and she hurried out into the hall. Standing at the front door was a delivery boy holding a large bouquet of roses exquisitely arranged and encased in cellophane.

'For me?' Karen queried uncertainly, and he grinned.

'If you're Karen Ingalls, they're for you.'

'Oh—thank you,' she added, nonplussed. There was a card tucked almost out of sight, and she carefully undid the cellophane to extract it.

Dearest Karen—all my love, Matt.

Her stomach performed a series of somersaults, and her eyes brightened suspiciously as she took down a vase large enough to hold them—two dozen, in all. She wanted to laugh and cry at the same time.

At seven-thirty when the telephone rang, she knew who it was even before she picked up the receiver.

'Karen? Matt,' the deep voice drawled close to her ear. 'How are you?'

'I'm fine,' she responded quietly. 'And you?'

His husky chuckle sent goosebumps scudding down her spine. 'How very polite—next you'll begin discussing the weather,' he mocked gently.

'Thank you for the roses—they're beautiful.'

'Like the girl to whom I sent them. Dare I ask if you miss me?'

'I've had a busy day,' she said irrelevantly, and he laughed. 'Shopping,' she elaborated.

'As long as you haven't been dabbling with a paintbrush, I shan't object. What did you buy?'

'Clothes—frocks for Lisa, and a few things for myself.'

'I'll demand an inspection when I come back—you can both get dressed up, and I'll take you out to dinner.'

'How is Christchurch?' she asked hesitantly.

'Cold—and lonely.'

Karen suddenly had difficulty in swallowing. 'No doubt you can remedy that,' she observed wryly.

'You impudent little kitten,' Matt derided softly. 'The minute I get my hands on you I'll kiss you until you beg for mercy.'

'I—I'd better go. Lisa is calling me,' she invented wildly, and heard his expressive sigh.

'Ah, Karen—the perfect excuse to escape. I'll ring you tomorrow.'

'I—there's no need.'

'There's every need,' Matt opined quietly. 'I regret every minute I'm away from you.'

'Don't—don't say things like that,' Karen said shakily.

'It happens to be true. Damn this distance,' he cursed bluntly. 'I can sense you backing into your protective shell again, and there's not much I can do about it from here.'

'Matt, you have to give me time to think,' she protested, and after a measurable silence he answered softly,

'I love you enough to want to give you the security of marriage before proving that, sexually, you have nothing to fear from me.'

'If you do—love me,' she struggled, 'don't rush things —*please*.' Her voice sounded pathetic and utterly forlorn.

'Karen,' he groaned huskily. 'For the love of heaven——'

'I have to go,' she broke in, on the verge of tears, and ignored his directive not to hang up by slowly replacing the receiver.

For over an hour she sat staring sightlessly at the flickering images on the television screen, her thoughts in chaotic turmoil. Twice the telephone rang, but she couldn't bring herself to answer it, and it was a further hour before she rose wearily to her feet and prepared for bed.

After depositing Lisa at school the following morning, Karen drove home with the intention of spending an hour or two in the garden. Her shoulder had improved measurably, and she didn't imagine the exercise would do it any harm.

She turned the Datsun into her driveway, and almost stopped breathing with shock at the sight of Matt's XJ-S Jaguar parked in front of the garage. Shakily she brought the car to a halt and slid slowly out from behind the wheel, her eyes riveting on his tall frame as he straightened and began moving towards her.

There was little she could tell from his expression, for it was deliberately bland. 'I thought you weren't due back until tomorrow.'

'I wasn't.' His eyes raked her slender frame attired in slacks and jumper, then settled with unnerving scrutiny on her expressive features. 'Why didn't you answer the phone, Karen?'

The softly-voiced query held an edge of steel, and she couldn't help the slight shiver of apprehension that feathered down her spine.

'Shall we go inside?'

Karen looked at him numbly, and allowed him to take her arm and lead her to the front door where he took the key from her nerveless fingers and inserted it into the lock.

In the lounge he stood apart, making no attempt to touch her.

'I'm due back at the airport in an hour—which gives me precisely thirty minutes before I have to leave, so I suggest you listen carefully to what I have to say.' He raked a hand through his hair, then dropped his arm in a gesture of weariness. 'There's only one way I can dispel your traumatic fear of sex. Talking about it won't achieve much, and as for giving you time,' he paused fractionally, then continued with disturbing significance, 'you've had six years. Giving you more time is being unnecessarily cruel. It all comes down to the relatively simple fact of whether or not you love *me*—

Matt Lucas. If you can't accept that I'll exercise gentleness and all the loving care at my command when I handle you in bed, then there's no point in attempting to continue our relationship. If you love, you trust—there can be no other way.' His eyes held hers unwaveringly. 'I'm not Brad, Karen.'

She wasn't capable of uttering a word, and after an interminable silence Matt thrust his hands into his trouser pockets and pinned her gaze.

'The next move has to be yours,' he directed quietly. 'I'll be back in Auckland the day after tomorrow, on the late afternoon flight. It will be up to you to let me know if we're to use the licence I've got and keep a three o'clock appointment with the register office the following day—or whether I must tear the licence in two.'

There was a dreadful finality about his words that was frightening, and she felt a cold hand clutch at her heart as he pulled back the cuff of his jacket and examined his watch.

'I must leave—I have to collect Ben, then drive to the airport.' He glanced down at her steadily. 'I won't ring, Karen. There isn't another thing I can add to what I've already said.'

Karen's eyes followed him across the room, and at the door he paused to look back at her.

'I love you,' he assured her gently. 'Remember that.'

She stood in the centre of the room, unable to move, and she stared fixedly at the wall as her jumbled thoughts vied for supremacy in a fight for sanity—as against total confusion. She'd been issued with an ultimatum, and she entertained no doubt that he meant every word.

Saturday. Oh dear God—that was only three days

away! How could she possibly think of getting married at all—let alone so soon? But if she didn't, she'd never see him again. Somehow that chilling thought slowly began to assume momentous proportion as the day progressed into evening, permitting no peace, and she lay in bed restlessly unable to sleep.

For much of Thursday Karen alternated between moments of clear decision and total uncertainty, and when the sun rose on Friday she was convinced she hadn't closed her eyes for more than a few minutes during the entire night.

Consequently, she felt like a worn-out dishrag—what was more, she looked like one! Her face was pale and her eyes wide with huge dark shadows beneath them. She couldn't eat anything, only nibbling on a slice of toast as she drank her coffee at breakfast, and she forwent lunch altogether.

'Mummy, aren't you feeling well?'

Karen switched off the engine and masked her expression with a warm smile as she turned towards the little girl. 'I'm fine, honey. I didn't sleep very well, that's all. Shall we go inside?'

Lisa picked up her school-bag and slid from the seat. 'I've got some pictures, and a notice. There's going to be a puppet show at school next week, and the teacher said we must bring the note back with some money if we're allowed to go. Can I, Mummy?'

'Yes, of course,' Karen replied absently. 'I'll get the money ready and sign the notice tonight, so that you can take it to school on Monday.' She reached into her bag for the keys, then remembered she still had them in her hand. Her powers of concentration weren't exactly to the fore at the moment, she decided ruefully as she inserted the front door key into the lock.

'Some biscuits and a glass of milk, Lisa?' she queried as she entered the kitchen, and she gave a fond smile as the little girl eagerly acquiesced.

When she had set the glass and biscuits down on to the table, she selected a chair and faced her daughter, unsure quite how to broach the subject that had been the cause of so much anguish and soul-searching over the past few days.

'You like Matt, don't you?' Karen began tentatively, and carefully watched Lisa's face for her reaction.

'He's nice—I like him a lot,' Lisa responded with poignant sincerity.

Now came the difficult part! 'What would you say if I told you Matt has asked me to marry him?' she queried quietly, and saw the steadily widening smile on her daughter's face.

'Has he?' Lisa cried with delight. 'Are you? Does that mean we'll go and live in his house with Mrs Rogers and Ben, and Barnaby?' She slid down from her chair and ran to fling her arms around Karen's waist. 'Oh, Mummy, you will marry him, won't you? There isn't anyone else I'd like for a daddy better than Matt.'

Karen clasped her arms around Lisa's small body and placed her cheek against the little girl's head. Such an emphatic acceptance! How wonderful it would be to live again in the uncomplicated world of a child. Everything was so simple—without foreknowledge of clouding doubts and anxieties.

'It won't be just the two of us any more, darling,' she cautioned gently. 'You're quite sure you won't mind having to share me with Matt?'

The tiny head shook back and forth. 'I'd like it real fine.'

Karen gave a shaky laugh. 'Well, in that case, I think I'd better get ready.' She lifted Lisa on to her lap and gave her a quick kiss. 'Matt arrives back in Auckland tonight, and I think it would be nice if I was at the airport when his plane comes in. Would you mind very much if I leave you with Barbara for a few hours? Matt and I will have a lot to talk about.'

'I can play with Tania,' Lisa concurred happily. 'When does the plane get in?'

'I'm not sure,' Karen had to admit. 'I'll ring and find out.'

The expected time of arrival of the flight from Christchurch was confirmed for five twenty-five, and Barbara, bless her, didn't question the reason behind Karen's sudden request to leave Lisa with her at such short notice.

The drive to the airport took longer than Karen anticipated, for the traffic flow was heavy, making for several stops at computer-controlled intersections along the way.

It was exactly five-thirty when she slid the car into a parking space adjacent to the domestic flight terminal, and she paused long enough to secure the lock before walking swiftly through the parking area towards the terminal exit. As she stepped from the pedestrian crossing she saw Matt's cream Jaguar slide to a halt and Ben emerge from behind the wheel. Then she caught sight of Matt himself.

Karen's heart seemed to thud loudly in her chest, and now that she was here, she felt oddly tentative about approaching him. He looked so—stern, almost grave, and her footsteps slowed to a gradual halt as she drew close.

'Hello, Matt.' Was that her voice—so low-pitched, it was scarcely more than a murmur?

In seeming slow motion she saw him turn, and the sudden flaring of warmth in those dark tawny eyes, the gentle widening of his mobile mouth, turned her bones to jelly.

'Karen,' he greeted huskily, and he leant out a hand to trail gentle fingers down her cheek towards the edge of her mouth.

There was no way she could stop her lips from trembling beneath his touch, and her eyes took on a shine from unshed tears as he cupped her face with his hands and gently lowered his head.

She gave a convulsive sob as his lips met hers, and she didn't offer any resistance when his arms enfolded her close against him. There was passion, leashed and in tight control, and she revelled in his embrace, the powerful quickening thud of his heartbeat as it kept time with her own, until he gently put her at arm's length.

'Did you come by car?'

She nodded. 'It's in the car park.'

'And Lisa?'

'I—she's with Barbara.'

His smile did strange things to her composure. 'Then let's collect her, and go home.' He took hold of her hand and spread her fingers between his. 'If you'll let Ben have your keys, he'll take your car. You're coming with me.'

Later that evening—much later, when she lay in bed in one of Matt's guest rooms on the verge of sleep, she could only view the preceding few hours with a hazy glow. Doubtless the several glasses of champagne she'd had to drink were partly responsible, but so much had happened she could hardly remember all of it.

First had come a telephone call to Grace, and much to Karen's surprise her mother had asked few questions —just given her assurance that she would be down the following morning in plenty of time for the wedding. Then had come dinner, during which an excited Lisa had chattered practically non-stop, and it was well after nine o'clock before Karen was able to put her to bed.

Then Matt had refilled her glass with more champagne and settled down on the sofa beside her. What happened after that became very hazy, for she could remember feeling drowsy, and the way her head kept slipping down against his shoulder, until he'd lifted her into his arms and carried her upstairs to bed. His kiss had been brief and teasingly gentle, then he had firmly withdrawn.

The last thing Karen could remember before falling asleep was looking at her watch and thinking that in fifteen and a half hours she would be Matt's wife.

CHAPTER NINE

THE wedding ceremony had seemed brief and impersonal, how many hours ago—five? Karen felt she had no sense of time. There had been photographs taken outside the register office, in the garden at Matt's home, and in the lounge. Champagne flowed both before and during the buffet-style dinner which had been prepared for the immediate family, and there had been more champagne when Mrs Rogers brought in an iced wedding cake.

Karen had chosen a dress of cream voile and teamed it with a waistcoat, knee-length boots and a shoulder-bag in contrasting tan. Needing every ounce of courage she possessed, she'd elected to wear her hair in a fashionable chignon in the hope it would lend her an air of sophistication.

In a matching cream dress and clutching a spray of orchids in her hand, Lisa looked positively adorable, and there was pure happiness in the smile she directed at each and everyone.

As for Matt—he looked immaculate and completely at ease in a dark pin-stripe suit, white silk shirt, and a dark elegantly-knotted tie.

Coffee was served at nine, and by ten o'clock everyone, including Grace who was taking charge of Lisa until the following evening, had left. Even Ann and Ben Rogers, after swiftly clearing away the remaining food, had discreetly retired.

'Another glass of champagne?'

Karen glanced up at the man standing less than a

foot away and shook her head in dissent. Already she was beginning to feel the effects of having sipped three glasses of the bubbly liquid over the past few hours, added to which she'd hardly been able to eat more than a few mouthfuls of food. She felt nervous—scared stiff, she amended with a mental grimace.

'Are you cold?'

She hadn't noticed she'd shivered. Oh lord, if only she could close her eyes and have the next few hours over and done with. 'I—no. Not really,' she found herself answering with as much calm as she could muster.

'I'll light the fire,' Matt indicated lazily, and he crossed to kneel before the wide brick hearth. The grate was already set, and within seconds the kindling flared. He added a few trimmed logs, tossed on some pinecones, and put up the spark-screen. Then he turned towards her and extended an arm.

'Come and sit down,' he directed, and like an automaton Karen obeyed him, settling herself very correctly on the cushioned sofa with her feet crossed at the ankles and her hands folded neatly in her lap.

The lighting slowly dimmed until only the softly-flickering glow from the fire illuminated the room, and as she stared into the flames a gentle swell of music flowed from concealed stereophonic speakers.

'I hope you like Streisand?'

Karen nodded silently, then her eyes widened measurably as Matt sat down beside her, and the startled glance she cast him revealed that he'd discarded his jacket, removed his tie, and loosened several buttons of his shirt. He looked thoroughly at ease, and she gave a nervous start as he reached for her hands.

Gently he separated them, spreading her fingers between his own, then he lifted her hand to his mouth and slowly kissed each finger in turn. As he leaned towards her she swallowed convulsively, and the instant his lips touched her cheek she opened her mouth with the intention of telling him she couldn't go through with it, but no words would come.

'You're beautiful, do you know that?' Matt said softly as he turned her face towards him. 'Eyes like the sea—so light and sparkling when you laugh, yet dark and unfathomable at times. Like now, when you're unsure and afraid.'

Her lashes fluttered down like a veil, and she edged the tip of her tongue over her trembling lips.

'Open your eyes,' he bade quietly.

Karen felt his fingers in her hair, loosening the pins that held the elaborate chignon in place, until it slowly unwound and tumbled down on to her shoulders.

'It's like golden silk,' he murmured, threading its length through his fingers. He touched his lips to each closed eyelid in turn, then gently trailed her cheekbone, down the edge of her jaw to her mouth, caressing her lower lip before beginning a gentle probing motion that caused her lips to part involuntarily.

It was a tantalising kiss that promised much, yet just as she ached for it to deepen, Matt trailed his lips down to begin a sensual exploration of the soft hollows at the base of her throat. Her whole body began to tingle with delicious sensations as his lips followed in the path of his hands as he slowly unbuttoned her dress and gently slid down the straps of her bra to expose first one creamy breast, then the other.

She felt an odd sense of loss as he slipped down to the floor, and her eyes flew wide as he released the zip of one boot. It slid off her foot to be followed by the other then he took hold of her hands and gently pulled her down beside him.

'I love you,' he vowed quietly. 'I want so much to make you part of me.'

'Matt——' Her protest died in her throat as his lips covered hers, gently at first, then becoming disruptively probing until she was lost beneath the sensual passion his touch evoked. Her whole body felt warm as a strange languor invaded her limbs, and she was scarcely aware of being divested of each remaining article of clothing until she felt the soft sheepskin rug beneath her bare skin.

'Matt—no——' Her eyes filled with fear as she began to struggle, and he gently pulled her into a sitting position.

'Undress me, Karen,' he bade huskily, his warm breath stirring a few stray tendrils of her hair, and she froze with shock.'

'I can't,' she whispered.

His eyes held hers, gently compelling. 'Yes, you can.' His hands closed over her shoulders as he leant forward to kiss her, and when he eventually raised his head she felt as if she was slowly drowning.

Shakily she reached out and undid the few remaining buttons on his shirt, then she pulled it free from his waist and slid it from his shoulders. Her hands trembled as they encountered the buckle at his waist, and he immediately covered them with his own. She closed her eyes as he began to help her, and a tide of embarrassment coloured her cheeks.

'Open your eyes, Karen,' Matt berated gently. 'I want you to see that it's me when I possess you—not some shadowy ghost from the past.'

Karen let her eyelids sweep slowly upwards, and of their own volition her lips began to tremble.

He caressed her then, until she felt on fire and ached for complete fulfilment, and she clung to him with unashamed abandon as he gently led her towards an ecstasy she hadn't imagined possible.

The logs in the grate had slowly burned away until only the glowing embers remained when Matt gently enveloped her slim body in the sheepskin rug, then he lifted her into his arms and slowly carried her upstairs, lingering often to bestow a fleeting kiss.

Karen's arms rose to encircle his neck, and she heard his husky chuckle as she buried her face against his throat. She wanted to cry from sheer happiness, and she was powerless to stop the silent trickling flow of tears as they wet her cheeks.

A wall-light glowed in subdued illumination in the bedroom at the end of the hallway, and his eyes darkened at the suspicious dampness that clung to her cheeks as he lowered her gently down on to the bed.

'Tears, Karen?'

Her eyes flew open and she searched his beloved face, seeing with a growing sense of wonder the seriousness and the slight hesitancy evident. 'Oh, Matt,' she breathed shakily. 'Matt, I love you,' she assured him softly, unable to tear her eyes from his as she reached up to draw his head down close to her own. 'So very much.'

His face slowly creased into a smile so warm she blushed beneath the passionate ardency of his gaze, and he gave a soft laugh as he nuzzled an earlobe, then let his lips begin a slow havoc-causing path down the length of her body.

'Sweet Karen,' he accorded gently. 'How many bad

moments you've given me over the past few days! You'll never know how hard it was for me to issue that ultimatum on Thursday morning. The rest of that day, and yesterday, I doubt I retained one lucid fact at any of the meetings I attended. Fortunately my secretary was there to take notes.' His eyes caressed her, then lingered on the softly-bruised mouth. 'You, my little witch, had rendered me incapable of any coherent thought, except one—if you would be at the airport to meet the plane.'

She couldn't resist teasing him a little. 'And if I hadn't?'

His eyes darkened and became immeasurably bleak. 'I think I would have resorted to caveman tactics,' he declared emotively.

'What about that *femme fatale*—Berenice?'

He gave a soft incredulous laugh. 'Darling, I'm no celibate—there have been several woman in my past.' His eyes darkened with passionate warmth as he said gently, 'But never has any one meant so much to me as you. You're the life of me—the very air that I breathe.'

Karen gazed up at him and whispered softly, 'I can't believe I had so many doubts.'

Matt leant out a hand and gently touched her lips. 'No regrets?'

She shook her head, then paused fractionally as a wicked gleam of laughter lit her eyes. 'Well, I can only think of one,' she began teasingly. 'You don't intend letting me sleep in this great bed alone, do you?'

His retribution was swift and fierce, and it was a long time before his lovemaking ceased and she lay drowsily in his arms. The past no longer had any meaning, and with the dawn it slipped into shadowy insignificance.

Harlequin Presents Collection

An exciting new series
of early favorites from

Harlequin Presents

This is a golden opportunity
to discover these best-selling beautiful
love stories — available once again
for your reading enjoyment...

because Harlequin understands
how you feel about love.

Harlequin Presents Collection

Available wherever Harlequin books are sold.

GREAT LOVE STORIES NEVER GROW OLD...

Like fine old Wedgwood, great love stories are timeless. The pleasure they bring does not decrease through the years. That's why Harlequin is proud to offer...

HARLEQUIN CLASSIC LIBRARY

Delightful old favorites from our early publishing program!

Each volume, first published more than 15 years ago, is an enchanting story of people in love. Each is beautifully bound in an exquisite Wedgwood-look cover. And all have the Harlequin magic, unchanged through the years!

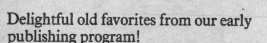

Two **HARLEQUIN CLASSIC LIBRARY** volumes every month! Available NOW wherever Harlequin books are sold.

FREE!

A hardcover Romance Treasury volume
containing 3 treasured works of romance
by 3 outstanding Harlequin authors...

...as your introduction to Harlequin's
Romance Treasury subscription plan!

Romance Treasury

...almost 600 pages of exciting romance reading
every month at the low cost of $5.97 a volume!

A wonderful way to collect many of Harlequin's most beautiful love
stories, all originally published in the late '60s and early '70s.
Each value-packed volume, bound in a distinctive gold-embossed
leatherette case and wrapped in a colorfully illustrated dust jacket,
contains...
- 3 full-length novels by 3 world-famous authors of romance fiction
- a unique illustration for every novel
- the elegant touch of a delicate bound-in ribbon bookmark...
  and much, much more!

Romance Treasury

...for a library of romance you'll treasure forever!

Complete and mail today the FREE gift certificate and subscription
reservation on the following page.

Romance Treasury

An exciting opportunity to collect treasured works of romance! Almost 600 pages of exciting romance reading in each beautifully bound hardcover volume!

You may cancel your subscription whenever you wish! You don't have to buy any minimum number of volumes. Whenever you decide to stop your subscription just drop us a line and we'll cancel all further shipments.